3|00

Bloody Mary
The Mystery of Amanda's Magic Mirror

Patrick Bone

For Virginia

The Overmountain Press

JOHNSON CITY, TENNESSEE

ISBN 1-57072-093-2
Copyright © 1999 by Patrick Bone
Printed in the United States of America
All Rights Reserved

1 2 3 4 5 6 7 8 9 0

To Amanda and her mom, Janet
To Juli and her mom, Kay

Contents

1

Something Hidden in the Attic

I never should have taken it. It wasn't like Mom hadn't warned me. Her meaning was clear enough: "Amanda, get your nose out of that box, now! I told you, leave it alone. It's going to the trash."

I thought that was funny since Mom never threw anything away. She either donated old stuff to charity or let me rummage through her junk to see what I could play with. Not this time. This time the box wasn't hers—it came out of the attic. I know because I found it there, right after we moved into the old house. Everyone called it the Butler mansion.

The house had two stories with an attic big enough for a third floor. I got the shivers the first time I climbed the narrow stairs and pushed open the creaky door that led into the attic. Talk about dark and damp! The only window opened out over the front yard. But with the giant pecan and black walnut trees and the scraggly hackberries hovering across the front of the house, not much daylight could filter through the window. "Perfect," I heard myself say. "Just right for having slumber parties and telling ghost stories."

Mom and my stepdad had driven by the "For Sale" sign in front of the house for three years. Sometimes I could hear them talk about how much fun it would be renovating an old mansion. They were sure it would cost too much for them to buy. But it never sold—no one even went to look at it. So when Mom's and my stepdad's curiosity got the best of them, they finally called the saleswoman. She couldn't come over soon enough.

I told Mom that the kids always said our house was

haunted. (Secretly that only made me want to live there more.) I loved old houses, especially houses with ghosts. Mom laughed about the ghost. She told me we were lucky to buy it so cheap.

"Besides," Mom said, "ghosts don't bother me."

That's why I was surprised when she freaked about the wooden box I found in the attic. Her face got all white, and her blue eyes seemed scared when she pried off the top of the box and looked inside.

"What is it, Mom?" The more scared she looked, the more I wanted to see.

"Nothing!" She slammed the top closed, picked up the hammer she had used to pry it open, and drove the nails back down. "Nothing you need to see, Miss Nebby Nose."

That's when I knew I had to find a way to get into that mysterious box.

2

The Mysterious Box

Someone had hidden it. That's why the box got my interest so. The other junk in the attic had been tossed about like someone had no use for it. Here and there, body parts lay scattered—doll body parts, I mean. An old tennis racket, strings busted, hung from a nail on the cracked, plaster wall. I stumbled across a chest of drawers with the drawers missing, and parts of dead bicycles lay scattered about as well. But the box was different.

Someone had taken care to hide it away from the other stuff. I discovered it when I opened a door to an unfinished part of the attic. It was so dark in there I almost missed it. But when my eyes adjusted, something resting across a couple rafters in a far corner caught my attention. Someone had hidden it with a faded Persian rug.

"That's funny," I whispered. "Must be something valuable in that old box, the way it's set aside, covered and all." I tried to lift it, but it was kind of heavy. I dragged and pulled it into the main attic and placed it in the center of the floor under the dim light bulb where I could see better. Words painted on one side read "Kentucky Sour Mash," and on the other side was a message scribbled in pencil, "Private property. Do not open."

My stepdad pursed his lips and cocked his head. "Kentucky sour mash?" He folded his newspaper and turned toward me, slipping his body a little sideways in the over-stuffed living room chair. His brown eyes got a little wider and he blew a few whiffs of brown hair from his glasses. "Why do you want to know about sour mash whiskey?" He still had on the dress shirt and tie he wore at the office where he worked as an accountant.

I always wondered if it hurt to wear his tie so snugly around his neck. When he turned his head, the skin squinched up in his shirt collar like someone had tied a noose around him and pulled on it. I got so distracted that I forgot his question and he had to repeat it.

"What's this about sour mash whiskey?"

I shrugged my shoulders and said, "Nothing. Just something I read on an old box."

He said, "Oh," and went on with his reading. I wasn't so lucky with Mom.

"What's that in your hand?"

She always did have the eyes of an eagle. I thought she wouldn't notice me since she was painting a landscape in her workroom next to the kitchen. She wore a blue smock with fresh paint smeared on it and on the tip of her nose. A touch of white brushed across the front of her short brunette hair. I did a double take, wondering if it was part of her latest 'do. A glance at the landscape told me no. The white was part of the clouds that hadn't made it to the canvas.

I felt kind of embarrassed and maybe just a little bit guilty that she had seen me take something out of the junk drawer. I tried to shield it with my body, but I was wearing my favorite cut-off jeans and a yellow halter top. My legs were too skinny to hide even something as small as a hammer.

Mom walked into the kitchen, brush in hand, just before I made it safely out of the parlor where my stepdad was still reading.

I could feel the ice in her blue eyes freezing the back of my head when she said, "I asked you, Miss Amanda, what's that in your hand?"

"Just a hammer, Mom." I smiled and started to walk off. That would have worked with my stepdad.

Mom knew me better than to let it go without an explanation. "Where are you going with that hammer, and what are you planning to do with it?"

When I was a little girl, I had tried lying. Big mistake. Mom could be a terror when I did something I shouldn't do, but lying about it only made the hidden monster in her come raging out. So, while I didn't lie, I did try to tell her the truth without letting the cat—or the monster—out of the bag. "Just going up to the attic to work on a project," I said.

The look on Mom's face said, *No way.* "What project?" She rolled her eyes and shook her head. "Never mind. I'll see for myself, thank you."

Of course, you already know the rest: Mom opened the box, got a weird look on her face, slammed the top back down, and told me not to touch the box because she was putting it in the trash.

That night, I had a hard time falling asleep in my upstairs room, just across the hall from Mom and my stepdad. I'd been reading a book about haunted houses, but I wasn't scared a bit. A little voice inside me asked if it wouldn't be a good idea to go downstairs for a glass of milk, a chocolate chip cookie, and maybe a peek on the back porch where the trash is kept.

My journey down the long, dark hallway and steep stairs seemed to take forever. Every floorboard in the old house creaked loudly enough to wake the dead. I wondered if the noise disturbed the resident ghost. I laughed, but stopped when I suddenly smelled something. Perfume? Maybe flowers? No...soap. Yes, I decided, bath soap. It smelled clean, fresh, but strange, and very old. I looked around and saw nothing, then I shrugged my shoulders and continued down the stairs.

When I finished my snack, I took a look toward the porch where Mom had put the box in the trash. Another little voice whispered, *Amanda, Mom said to leave that box alone.* I really wish I'd listened to that voice.

3

The Terrible Revelation

I figured I had earned a peek into the box. Yuck! Ever try fishing something out of the trash? Wet stuff! I tried not to see what it was that slithered across my fingers like slime. It smelled like...like garbage. Yuck!

The box opened easily enough because Mom had already loosened the nails. A couple still squeaked when I pulled at the top. I worried that someone upstairs would hear the noise and think someone downstairs was doing something she shouldn't be doing. Of course, that someone would be right.

There wasn't much light in the mud room, only the moon shining through the latched screen door. I was really on the back porch, but being in the mountains and all, back porches are called mud rooms because that's where you take off your wet coats and overshoes during bad weather. It was early fall—not cold enough to have to wear a coat outside. Still, for some reason I had the shivers. I wondered why Mom had closed the box so suddenly. Would I be as afraid as she of whatever was in there?

Only one way to find out. I reached across the box with both hands to finish prying off the cover. Suddenly a gust of wind blew through the screen door and whistled around the old porch, blowing against the sleeves of my pajamas like some unseen presence trying to tell me, *Don't do it, Amanda, don't open that box.* At least that's the message my mind heard.

The wind stopped just as suddenly as it had come. I became aware of that smell again. Soap? Like something my grandmother would use in her bath.

I had second thoughts about opening the box. For a moment, I wondered if maybe I should just forget it. "Nawwwww," I heard myself whisper as I lifted the cover off very slowly. Even then, my imagination said, *You'll be sorry.* I half expected something to jump out of the box and attack me.

Something did come out, causing me to shiver a little. But it wasn't what I had imagined. It was an odor, different from the clean one I had smelled earlier. I thought of my grandmother's moldy old trunk where she stored keepsakes she'd saved since she was a little girl. That thought didn't bother me, but another one did. It crossed my mind that maybe the smell was like the inside of a coffin.

"Stop it, Amanda," I whispered. "You're just scaring yourself for no good reason." With that, I lowered my head toward the box and looked inside. Mom would have been proud of how fast I slammed the top back down.

My blood turned cold and every inch of my body shivered.

"You didn't see that," I said.

Then, I took a deep breath and answered myself, "Yes, you did, Amanda, you saw it. You saw...the face. The face of...." I couldn't let my mouth say what I'd seen with my eyes. That didn't stop the fear. What I had seen was alive. A face! An ancient, ugly face. The face of a monster.

4

Like Eating Potato Chips

Have you ever done something you said you would never do again, and then you decided to do it one more time? Like eating just one more potato chip? That's what happened out there on that dark, creaky porch. I had looked into the box and seen something horrible, ugly, so frightening I wanted to run. But a part of me said, *Look again, Amanda.*

And I said, "Oh well."

I could feel the goose bumps rise all over my body as I pulled back the top of the wooden box. The wind started to blow again, even harder than before, like nature itself was trying to tell me not to be foolish. Somewhere in the night, a dog howled. Another took up the mournful cry, then another. Behind me, something seemed to move, and I was sure my mom had discovered what I was up to. When I slowly turned around, I saw nothing except moon shadows from the trees shivering in the wind. "Do it now," I said aloud.

I lifted the top slowly and saw...a mirror.

I sighed so loud I thought the whole neighborhood could hear me. "It was ME!" I said out loud, "ME in the mirror!"

What an imagination, I thought, as I picked up the mirror and looked into it. Sure enough there was no monster there, only me. Even though my ex-boyfriend, Gerald Grandhopper, said I was a monster, what I saw in that beautiful jeweled mirror was only me.

Fact is, instead of looking like a monster, I looked better than I could remember looking. Even in the dark, my eyes shined like the bluest sky I'd ever seen, and my hair, always dirty blonde, now had gold and red highlights in it and looked like it had just been washed and rinsed at the beauty shop.

"This is great," I said.

I should have known something was wrong with that picture. But what girl in her right mind would suspect something wrong with looking ravishingly beautiful?

I suppose a hidden part of my mind did say, *Amanda, isn't this a bit strange?* But the biggest part of me said, *Uhhh. Duhhh, oh well.*

A careful search of the box revealed nothing else of interest. I found a few old scarves and some wool sweaters in drab colors. I was sure they would look better in the Goodwill Store than my bedroom chest of drawers. I put the mirror aside, covered the box, and put it back into the garbage slime. "There," I said, "Mom will never know."

But as I picked up the mirror, the wind started to blow again. I could swear I heard it say, "Don't keep it, Amanda!"

5

Magic

But I did keep it. I took the mirror upstairs to my bedroom and played with it all night. I decided it must be a magic mirror, because whenever I looked into it, I became whatever I imagined. If I wanted to be a princess I closed my eyes and opened them to find myself dressed in the finest royal garments complete with jewels and servants.

"You're a trapeze artist," I said, and in the mirror I saw myself swinging from the center ring of the circus. I wore gold sequined tights, and my hair was pulled back in a ponytail, which flew through the air behind me as I twisted and tumbled as many times as I wanted and still reached the safety of the bar.

By now, I found myself wondering how all this was possible. I blamed it on my imagination. Mom always said I had a freaky imagination, so I was sure that's all it was. Still, I couldn't wait to share the mirror with someone. It had to be someone who wouldn't make fun of me, so I made a list.

My very, very best friend, Megan? She would be great, but she moved away and went to another school, and I didn't see her so often anymore.

Jessica Heathcliff, my next best friend? I shook my head. Much too duh. Jessica would look into the mirror and see...Jessica.

Josie Garcia? Blabbermouth. Everyone would hear about it, and I'd be accused of being crazy.

Juli Kelley, my stepsister? Hmmmmmmmm? Even though she's older then me, she always plays fair, even Barbies. In fact, she was my favorite and only Barbie playmate. Juli had an imagination almost as freaky as mine. We both knew we couldn't reveal our secret, playing Barbies, that is. Sometimes I pretended I would be able to play with dolls forever. Juli didn't laugh at me when I told her that.

I whispered, "Juli. I'll show the mirror to Juli this weekend when Dad comes to pick me up."

I looked into the mirror and said, "Oh, Juli, you'll just love this." I smiled and saw the most beautiful smile I could ever imagine. Then something really strange happened. Suddenly, my face turned into Juli's face.

"Cool!" I couldn't take my eyes off the mirror.

That's when something else happened. It wasn't strange this time. More like awesome. No, the word is scary.

Slowly, very slowly, Juli's beautiful smile turned into an ugly grimace. The longer I looked into the mirror, the uglier her face became. Her soft brown eyes changed to green with jagged red lines shooting out like bloody bolts of lightning. Her smooth face wrinkled in front of my eyes. Where she had braces, she now had crooked teeth that were stained and cracked. I tried to look away, but I couldn't.

All of a sudden the image seemed to come out of the mirror and grow closer to my face. She belched a horrible smell, like something had died, worse than the odor from the box. Drool oozed out the sides of her mouth and down her chin. I saw her tongue, black, swollen, and pitted. The grotesque face hovered inches from mine, and it smiled—an evil, threatening smile. I heard a low raspy growl I realized was a voice.

"Hungry," it said. "I'm soooo hungry."

I screamed, and the louder I screamed, the closer the face came to mine, still laughing and saying, "Hungry, soooo hungry!"

In spite of my cries, the image edged closer still. Suddenly, I saw arms come out from the mirror, arms with thick black curly hair. The hands looked crooked and twisted with long pointed fingernails, thick and curved like claws. My body felt paralyzed. The hands grabbed me by my shoulders and pulled me toward the face, which said, "Now I will eat you!" Her jagged teeth touched my throat. I imagined their sharp edges piercing my skin and warm blood dripping down my neck.

I closed my eyes and screamed, "MOOOOMMMMMYYY!"

6

Just a Dream?

When I opened my eyes, Mom was there, holding me by the shoulders and telling me everything was okay. "You had another dream, honey," she said.

When I stopped crying enough to see, I looked over at my dresser and saw the magic mirror where I must have put it before I fell asleep. Just as quickly I looked back, hoping Mom wouldn't notice. "Oh, Mom," I said. "I just had the dumbest dream."

She smiled back. "You always do, Amanda. You always do." She gave me a big hug. "Now we've got to get you ready; it's almost eight in the morning. Your dad will be here soon for your weekend visit."

I smiled. "Boy, do I have a scary story to tell Juli!"

7

My Other Home

The ride to Dad's place took only an hour. I used to think it was all day, but now that I am older, I look forward to the trip and the chance to talk to Dad and catch up on all the gossip about Juli.

Dad's beard had turned gray, and it made him look ancient. I never would have told him that, though I doubt it would have bothered him. He was a writer and had an okay personality—for a father. He talked about the newest story he was working on and mentioned the party Juli had planned for Halloween. "Of course, you're invited," he said.

That made me feel good. Even though Dad was always telling me how he loved me and how much everyone enjoyed my visits, I still felt a little left out at times. Juli went out of her way to make me feel wanted. She was there to greet me when we arrived. "Just in time to help empty the dishwasher," she said.

What a way to make me feel wanted. But I didn't mind. Juli and her mom, Kay, never made special allowances for me when I visited. If I was going to be one of the family, I had to act like one. Even if that meant doing chores and picking up after myself.

Halfway through the bottom tray of the washer, Juli had a great idea. "Let's put on Mom's makeup," she whispered. We laughed just as Kay walked into the kitchen.

She had on her white shorts and a tee shirt, and wore the reading glasses she said were made out of the bottom of Coke bottles. I could see some kind of medical journal in one hand and a pen in the other. Like my mom, Kay is a nurse. I figured I'd never have to worry about not being sent to the doctor for a sore throat in either home. Another advantage is an unlimited access to books with pictures of people with all kinds of gruesome diseases, which grosses me out even if I can't take my eyes off them. That's when I decided I'd be a scientist when I grew up.

Juli wanted to be a music teacher. She played the saxophone in a jazz band and the accordion in a...well, in an accordion band. I told her it was good she had decided to teach music, because she would make a terrible beauty consultant. She wasn't very good with the makeup. I was worse.

We played in her room, trying hard not to give ourselves away by screaming at the faces we made in her vanity. Juli's lips looked vampire red and twice as large as they were before she smeared herself with the lipstick. I tried to make my eyes look bigger the way I watched my mom do. For some reason it didn't work. Juli said I could pass for a blonde-headed raccoon. Very funny from someone who looked like The Lips monster.

We screamed every time we looked at each other. Then we looked in the mirror and screamed some more. You can imagine the surprise on Kay's face when she walked into Juli's bedroom and said, "What's going on in here?"

We stopped, frozen in place, Juli's hand with a mascara brush still touching her eyelashes, and I with another piece of evidence in my hand.

Kay's mouth hung wide open.

Juli and I expected the worse. Instead, her mom broke out laughing. Juli and I looked back at each other in the mirror and started laughing, too. Pretty soon, all three of us were laughing and screaming so loud my dad walked in.

Silence.

He only got a "WHAT?" out of his mouth before he started laughing too.

Kay got serious for a moment and told Juli the makeup was coming out of her allowance. Then my dad and Kay left. I guess we had gotten too gross even for open-minded grownups.

I was so excited with my makeover, I almost forgot the

magic mirror in my backpack. "Juli," I said, "you won't believe what I have to show you."

She batted her mascaraed eyelashes and said, "Oh yeah?"

By then I had dumped half my clothes out of the pack and found the mirror I had put there a few hours earlier.

"Ta-ta!" I held it in front of me, checking out my makeup.

"Cool," Juli said, "like cool, I mean like it's...why, it's...wait a minute, don't tell me. Yes! It's a mirror! Amanda how could you ever wait so long to show me?"

"Just you wait, Miss Sarcasm of the Entire Universe, just you wait till you find out what this magic mirror can do for you."

Juli squinched up her mouth and turned to her vanity, ignoring me while she made faces in the mirror. I wanted to tell her to look in my mirror and see how beautiful she was. But that's not what I said. Instead something strange came over me and I said, "Look in the mirror and say 'Bloody Mary' thirteen times."

I did a double take. *That's not what I wanted to tell her,* I thought. So I tried again, and the words came out the same: "Look in the mirror and say 'Bloody Mary' thirteen times."

8

I Dare You

From there on, things didn't get any better. Every word out of my mouth just made it worse.

"Go ahead, I dare you," I said to Juli. "Look into the mirror and say 'Bloody Mary' thirteen times. Of course, if you're a chicken...."

"I'm not a chicken," Juli responded. "I'm just not a child, like you."

She was two whole years older than me. But she was also my very best friend in the world, even if we only saw each other every other weekend. I couldn't understand what was happening.

"I am not a child," I said back to her. "I'll show you! I'm not afraid to say 'Bloody Mary' in the mirror. Here, I'll show you," I said. I started to lift the mirror.

"Never mind, Amanda." Juli took the mirror from my hand and held it in front of her face.

"You know the story," I reminded her.

"Of course I do," she answered. "I've known it lots longer than you. If you look into a mirror and say 'Bloody Mary' thirteen times, you'll turn into a monster or something."

"And the only way to reverse the spell is to say 'Bloody Mary' once in the mirror, in the dark," I added.

"Okay, silly," she said, "I'm ready. Prepare yourself for the most totally awesome monster you'll ever meet. You count.

"Bloody Mary."

"One."

"Bloody Mary."

"Two."

"Bloody Mary."

"Three."

I didn't believe in that dumb story any more than Juli did. But none of the kids I'd played with had ever tried it. Juli was the first, including me. Once, I looked in the bathroom mirror and started saying "Bloody Mary." I stopped at twelve. I told myself it was stupid and I shouldn't bother about it. But I guess I was just a little scared.

"Bloody Mary."

"Thirteen!"

"There. It's done. Now, Amanda, see what a silly kids' story this is?"

Before I could answer, Juli got a mean look on her face. She bent over, low to the ground, and started to growl.

Juli, are you okay? I tried to say. But I couldn't get the words out.

"BOO!" she yelled. "Fooled you, didn't I?" she laughed. "Na, na, na, na, na, na, Amanda believes in monsters, Amanda believes in monsters.... "

"Forget it," I said. "Let's play Barbies."

I knew that would get her. Even at her advanced age she still liked to play Barbies. I was her only Barbie playmate. She would have died if her classmates had seen her. But somehow, with my being her stepsister and all, it didn't seem to matter.

We played till late.

Finally, Dad said, "Time to go to bed."

Bed was the basement. We kids slept there because it was lots cooler, and kind of spooky. But the real reason was so my dad and Juli's mom couldn't hear us play and carry on all night long. The only problem was, there were no lights down there. We had to lay out our sleeping bags before dark. When we went to bed, we would play with the flashlight and talk or tell stories till we fell asleep. That night Juli and I told ghost stories. We stopped when the flashlight batteries went dead. But I wasn't afraid.

Not long after I fell asleep, I woke to a strange sound coming from right next to me. It was Juli. She was talking in her sleep or something. She sounded very uncomfortable.

"Juli," I asked, "are you okay?"

No answer.

"Juli?" Still no answer.

Then I heard her moan. I thought she was having trouble breathing.

"Juli?" I called out again.

"I'm not Juli," a voice answered. It didn't sound like Juli. It was low and growly and totally bad.

"Oh, come on," I said, "cut it out. You can't fool me twice." There was no response, just a scratching on the side of my sleeping bag.

"Stop it, Juli! You're scaring me!"

She stopped. Then, slowly, the scratching started again.

"That's enough," I said, as I reached out to push her. That was a big mistake. Instead of Juli's nice warm arm, I touched something extremely furry and cold. I froze. "Juli, please stop this," I whispered.

"I'm not Juli," that terrible voice said again. I heard something reach toward me. By this time, only the top of my head was sticking out of my sleeping bag. I felt long pointy things, like claws, run through my hair.

"Hungry," she growled.

"DADDY!" I screamed as loud as I could. I scrambled out of the sleeping bag. The only thing that saved me was that the thing also had to get out of her sleeping bag. She was much slower than me. I could hear her grunting like an old woman and scratching like a monster. By this time, I was screaming, "DADDY!" louder than ever. But he didn't come...and she did.

"I'm so hungry," I heard her say. "I haven't eaten in a hundred years! I'll gobble your nose and nibble on your ears."

Oh gosh, I thought, *I'm going to be eaten by my stepsister! Even Cinderella didn't have to go through that!*

"DADDY!"

9

Bloody Mary

The door at the top of the basement stairs opened.

"Amanda?" It was Dad! I felt so relieved. Now I would be saved!

"You kids settle down, right now. Hear me?"

"Daddy!" I screamed, "Juli said 'Bloody Mary' thirteen times and turned into a monster with furry arms and claws and now she's trying to eat me!"

"Sure," Dad yelled back. "Now get to sleep, or else!" The door slammed. I was alone again.

Dead meat, I thought. *Now what do I do?* The thing was still between me and the stairs. It was so dark that I couldn't see where she was. But that worked to my advantage. Every time she moved, I heard her and moved away. Trouble was, she stayed between me and the stairs so I couldn't run for it. It was only a matter of time before she caught me. I had to do something.

The mirror! I remembered: To change the monster back to a human, you must get her to say "Bloody Mary" into the mirror in the dark. But where was that mirror? And how would I find it with the monster trying to eat me?

I needed a plan to distract her long enough to feel on the floor for the mirror. It's somewhere near my sleeping bag, I remembered.

The closet! That's it! Trying not to make a sound, I felt along the wall for the closet. The monster moved. I stopped. Was she reading my mind? I could hear her breathing, low and raspy, like she was struggling to move.

At last! I felt the closet door. Slowly, very slowly, I turned the doorknob until I felt the catch release. Then I swung the door open and yelled as loud as I could, "You can't catch me in here!" I slammed the door shut without going in, hoping the monster would think I was trying to hide in the closet.

She started in my direction, away from the sleeping bags. "You can't hide from me in there," she growled. "I'm so hungry. I would love a little girl right now. I haven't eaten in a hundred years. I'll gobble your nose and nibble on your ears. But don't worry, dearie. After a while, you'll probably pass out and won't even know what I'm doing to you!"

I just about lost it then and there. But I knew I had to find the mirror. As the thing edged toward the closet, I crawled on the floor near the sleeping bag, feeling everywhere for the mirror. *There! No. That's a Barbie garage. It's here somewhere—I hope!*

I heard her at the closet. There was a sharp scratching sound on the door like she was trying to find the knob, then the squeak of the doorknob turning slowly, but not quietly. The door opened and I heard the monster shuffle. I could imagine her setting herself to catch me as I tried to flee. Then I heard the rustle of clothes and boxes.

"Where are you?" she whispered like a cat toying with a mouse. She got louder and screamed, "Tricked!" She slammed the door and turned to announce, "I'll get you for that! And I won't be nice this time. I will be fed. I haven't eaten in a hundred years. I'll gobble your nose and nibble on your ears. I'm coming for you, dearie."

She walked straight in my direction. I wanted to run for the stairs, but I knew I had to break the spell. I couldn't do it by running away. I had to face the monster and get her to talk into the mirror. After all, she was once my stepsister!

I still hadn't found the mirror. I began to grope wildly on the floor. Barbie toys. *If I never see another Barbie toy....* Suddenly, she was directly in front of me. I held my breath. She stopped. I could feel the wind from her hairy arms fanning the darkness right over my head.

I won't give up without a fight, I determined, as I searched for something to use as a weapon. *Ah, something hard and skinny. I can stab with it. Oh no, this can't be happening.*

Bloody Mary's about to attack me and I'm going to defend myself with...with Ken?

In desperation, I flung the doll at her and missed. It hit the wall behind her. She turned with a jerk. "You'll have to be quieter than that," she whispered, moving in the direction of the sound. As she shuffled away, I allowed myself to breathe again and continued my search.

Finally! I touched the mirror. Can I still do this? Well, it's now or never!

Opening my mouth, I forced out the words, "I'm here."

"Wait for me, dearie," she answered. I could hear her shuffle closer. She was still breathing heavily. Every step she took, she would say, "Hungry, soooo hungry." Suddenly, she was standing right in front of me. I heard her moan.

But where, I wondered, *where should I hold the mirror?* Her breath directed me. *Ugh. Don't monsters know about toothbrushes?*

"Please," I begged, "before you eat me, can you tell me your name?"

"Why, of course, dearie, you know me," she said with a cackle.

"I'M BLOODY MARY."

There, I did it! It's over! She's changed!

"And I'm going to eat you, NOW!"

She didn't change!

I screamed like it was the very last thing I was going to do on this Earth, and I wanted to make it last, "DAAAAAAAAD-DDDDDDDDDYYYYYYYYY!!!"

The basement door burst open. "Amanda, I told you—" Before Dad finished his sentence I was halfway up the stairs.

"Oh, Daddy, Daddy, please, please. Bloody Mary's going to eat me. Call the police, call the fire department, let's get out of here. I want my Mommy!"

"Amanda, stop that NOW." Dad meant business. "You've had a bad dream. I'll just go down with you and tuck you back into bed."

"NO! No, please, Daddy, no. The monster, Juli, the monster, please!"

"Okay, okay," he reassured me. "I'll go down myself and

show you everything is okay." Still crying, I stayed at the top of the stairs ready to go for help as soon as Dad screamed. But he didn't. Instead he called to me, "Amanda. Come down here. Now!"

10

Just Another Bad Dream?

Is he crazy? I thought. With every step down, I imagined seeing the monster rage up to eat me. Instead, at the bottom of the stairs Dad spotted his flashlight on Juli's angelic face. She was sleeping like a baby in her sleeping bag.

"But, Dad," I tried to explain. He cut me off.

"You've had a bad dream, honey," he assured me. "Now get back into your sleeping bag. We'll talk in the morning. And please, no more noise. We all need our sleep."

It was my turn to mean business. Wiping tears and snot with one hand, and pointing my finger up at Dad with the other, I declared, "Daddy, if you try to make me stay down here with Juli, I promise nobody in this house is going to get any sleep at all tonight." When I finally fell asleep, it was on the living room couch.

Dad woke me in the morning to get packed for the trip back to Mom's house. He didn't have to tell me twice. Going downstairs for my stuff wasn't nearly as scary as it had been in the dark. At the bottom, I peeked around the stairwell. Juli was already awake. She was combing her long brown hair in the mirror. "Morning," she said. "Sleep okay? You tossed and turned all night. When I woke up, you were already upstairs. Hope you're all right."

I didn't answer. *Was it really just a dream after all?* I wondered.

Juli smiled. "I know! Let's play Bloody Mary. You count," she said, looking into the mirror.

"Never!" I screamed, ripping the mirror out of her hand. While she sat there stunned, I walked over to the corner and threw it into the trash can. I paused, looking at the broken pieces of glass. That's when I heard the voice again, behind me.

"You shouldn't have done that, dearie," the voice rasped. "Seven years bad luck, you know. Starting now!"

I froze. I couldn't move if I had wanted to.

"Who, who's there?" I asked.

"Why, it's Bloody Mary! And I'm still very hungry. I haven't eaten in a hundred years. I'll gobble your nose and nibble on your ears. For breakfast!"

My fate was sealed. Slowly, I turned to meet the monster about to eat me. There stood my stepsister, Juli, with a great big grin on her face, holding her favorite stuffed toy, Tiger, with its big furry legs and long, sharp plastic claws.

"BOO!" she said. "Tricked you again."

I was so relieved I forgot to get mad. Instead I hugged her and said, "Oh Juli, I love you." She must have thought I was crazy, because all she did was stand there looking surprised.

"Five minutes," Dad yelled. I ran to pack my clothes and Barbies and my jacket which I saw over by the closet door. I crossed the room and was just about to bend over to pick up the jacket when something caught my eye.

"Scratches," I gasped. On the door, near the knob, were several long, deep scratches. Embedded under a splinter were tufts of short, dark, curly hair and what looked to be a piece of broken...claw. *Is this real, or another trick?* I wondered as I reached to touch the bits of hair.

"What are you doing?" Juli asked, standing immediately behind me. I turned with a jerk hoping my back was big enough to cover the evidence.

"Nothing. Just getting my stuff," I lied. Juli smiled innocently.

She pulled me to her in a great big tight hug. Then she kissed me and whispered lovingly in my ear, "See you in two weeks...dearie!"

11

Would You Believe....

At first Mom looked at me like she thought I had made a bad joke. "Very funny, Amanda. Juli is Bloody Mary. You're joking, right?"

I shook my head. "No, Mom, honest, cross my heart. It's the truth, Mom. Last night, Juli turned into Bloody Mary. Please, please, I really do need to talk to you."

Her smile turned into a frown. She still had on her nursing uniform from work, and ordinarily she would have told me to wait till she changed into jeans and a sweatshirt. This time, she took my hand and led me into the living room where we sat together on the couch. She smiled at me and said, "Come closer, honey. I want to give you a hug." I heard a hesitation in her voice. She put her arms around me, but I could tell she was testing my forehead for a fever or something.

I said, "You don't believe me, do you?" I still had my backpack in my hands and felt too hot in my jeans and the flannel shirt Dad told me to put on for the trip home. I wondered if maybe the shirt made me feel warm and Mom thought I was sick or something. You know how moms are. Double that when you're living with a mom who is also a nurse.

I looked up at her and said, "Well, do you believe me?"

Mom took a deep breath and let it out with a sigh. "Yes, ah well...I do believe you believe it." She struggled for something else to say, then added, "You say it happened at night? Last night? Juli turned into...Bloody Mary?"

I nodded.

She took another deep breath and sighed again. I found

myself wishing she wouldn't do that. She said, "Honey, you know how bad your dreams are."

I nodded. "But this time...."

"Remember the time you dreamed that you climbed a ladder and found the zipper to the sky?"

"Uh huh." Darn, I wished she hadn't reminded me of that one. Moms never forget anything...never.

She recalled every detail. "Remember when I came into the bedroom? You were screaming, "Mommy, Mommy open the window so the water can run out and we won't drown."

This time I sighed. "But, Mom...."

"You said it was real then, too. Just like you say Bloody Mary is real. You said you wouldn't be able to go back to sleep because your bed was floating in the water."

She had me. I did believe that dream was real. It was so real I could see the water and all, even splash it with my hands. I saw both my cats float by, meowing for me to save them. When I woke up the next morning, I was surprised to find my room all dry. When I went to breakfast that day, Mom reminded me about the dream. "You just had a bad dream, honey," she said. Exactly the way Dad told me I was dreaming about Blood Mary. Wow! Now I felt really scared.

I hugged Mom harder. With my head snuggled against her, I mumbled, "I'm scared, Mommy."

She patted my back. "I'll see what I can do, baby." She held me tighter, kissed the top of my head and kept me in her arms for a long time. I wanted to cry, but something inside told me I better save it. Was I ever confused.

Mom got up from the couch and said, "Why don't you go outside and play or find something to read in your room?" She had a serious look on her face. "On second thought, maybe you ought to be careful what you're reading," she said. "I'll get back with you in a little while. Something I need to check out first."

She walked upstairs toward her bedroom. When she reached the top of the stairs, she looked down at me and smiled. Uh-oh. That's when I knew something was seriously wrong. Mom never smiled like that when there was good news.

I waited till I heard her door close before I crept up the stairs. It took forever since every step creaked like someone was following just behind me. When I finally got to her door, I could hear Mom talking.

It occurred to me there was no reason to disturb Mom just then, so I sort of listened in on her conversation. She said, "Yes. Uh huh. I think it's gotten worse lately. Uh huh. Uh huh. No. Well, I guess I could bring her down. Yes. Yes. No. Uh huh. If you really think so. Uh huh. I never thought it could lead to that. You really mean the hospital?"

I almost lost it then and there. I'm being committed to the hospital? My stomach sank and I felt like finding a place where I could hide forever and ever. *You're going to be sick*, I said to myself. I wanted to run somewhere. Run where? Dad? He thinks I'm dreaming, too. Suddenly, it hit me. Maybe they're right? Maybe I am crazy, did dream it, or made it all up in my mind somehow?

As I stood there coming to the conclusion that I was crazy, the door opened and Mom stood over me. She wasn't smiling this time.

I felt the tears burn my eyes. A feeling came over me like I was in a schoolroom and all the kids were laughing at me and making fun of me. I turned and ran to my room, slammed the door, crawled on my bed, and buried my head in my stuffed toys. They were my friends. Ever since I was a little girl, my stuffed toys had been my friends. I needed them just then. I needed any kind of friend I could find.

12

Doctor Smiles

He looked down at me, a plastic smile frozen on his face. The desk in front of him was as big as an airport runway, so tall I could barely see his face over it. When I entered the office he pointed his long skinny finger toward a chair and said, "Sit there!"

It was a soft green leather chair, cushy. The second I sat down I started sinking into it and had the idea it might eat me up. The more I tried to get comfortable, the deeper I sank.

Doctor Smiles wasn't his real name. That's the name Rebecca gave him. I'll tell you more about her in a minute. Doctor Smiles's real name was Ringleheim, Dr. Heinreid P. Ringleheim. That's what the name on his door said. But I think Doctor Smiles fit him better. He had on a dark green pinstripe suit with a vest where he kept a gold watch he looked at before he started asking me questions.

His coal black hair distracted me. It was slicked back, almost pasted there on his pointed head. I wondered what his pillow looked like when he woke up in the morning. He probably didn't even have to comb his hair after he showered. Nothing, not even water, could seep through that stuff.

His nose looked long and thin, and it was shaped like a hook. Long black hairs grew from his nostrils. They were the only hairs on the thin face that seemed to be mostly skin and skeleton—and smile. Let's not forget the smile.

It was that same day at dinner in the hospital cafeteria that Rebecca warned me about him. Mom had dropped me off at the hospital only minutes earlier—what a way to spend a Saturday afternoon. When Mom kissed me goodbye, there were tears in her eyes. The nurse who checked me in grabbed the first girl she saw and said, "Rebecca here will show you around."

We sat in the cafeteria. It was a large white room with no windows. There was nothing on the walls, and the noise from the kids eating and talking at the same time bounced around the room like a really bad air band. Everything smelled like antiseptic soap. Except for the food. The food smelled like plastic—runny plastic. I sat at a table with two other girls and Rebecca. The other girls ignored me, while Rebecca smiled at me like a cat that ate the bird.

"Gonna see Doctor Smiles." She didn't ask me; she told me.

I said, "Huh?" in between a bite of runny chicken pot pie that had more run in it than chicken or pie.

"Doctor Smiles," she repeated. "You're a weekender, right?"

I nodded my head.

"Not me," she said, "I'm an inmate." She had on a plain brown dress that was almost as unappealing as the one I wore in Brownie Scouts. Her hair was brown too, just like her twinkling eyes. I would have died having to wear another uniform. I had on my jeans and a Colorado Rockies sweatshirt. My jaw was set—they won't get me in one of those without a fight.

I decided not to ask Rebecca what *inmate* meant, thinking it would have been too personal a question to ask. Wrong!

Rebecca said, "Don't you want to know what an inmate is?"

"Yes!" I couldn't wait to hear, since it sounded really dangerous—or something like that.

She got a big smile on her face, revealing teeth almost as crooked as mine. Then she looked around like she was trying to make sure no one was looking. "An inmate is an incorrigible."

I gasped, holding my hands to my heart. She laughed.

"No!" I said.

We both laughed.

She said, "Bet you don't know what an incorrigible is."

I said, "No."

We both laughed again, loud enough so everyone stared

at us.

Across the dining room, a voice said, "Keep it down over there." I looked up and saw someone dressed in white sitting at a table by the door. She was a large woman, much older than my mother. Her hair was dyed blue and tied up in the back. Heavy blue makeup surrounded her blue eyes, which focused on us for a while.

Rebecca smiled at her. "That's nurse Cronkite," Rebecca whispered. "She's harmless. Watch." The nurse went back to a paperback novel whose cover showed a woman with great big bosoms and long, wavy blonde hair. A wild looking he-man, whose shirt was opened so you could see his hairy chest, knelt at the woman's feet.

"She reads a new one of those every day," Rebecca said, "mostly when she's supposed to be keeping us from laughing and having fun."

"What's incorrigible mean?" I whispered, getting back to the subject.

"It means I don't get along with the doctors, the other staff people, and mainly, my parents."

"Why?" I asked.

"Because my parents are divorced."

"Whose aren't?"

"That's not the point. My parents are divorced and act like they're still married and hate every minute of it. Guess who they use to beat on each other with?"

I shook my head. "I'm lucky, I guess. My parents try to work things out. They argued a little about whether I should come here or not, but mom agreed that if the doctor cleared me, I wouldn't have to stay for more than this weekend."

"I wouldn't want you to stay either," she said. Her eyes turned sad, and I knew she would have liked a special friend.

Then, she smiled again. "Okay, here's how to go home, if that's what you really want."

I smiled and she knew my answer.

She said, "What you got to do is go along with Doctor Smiles. Just agree with him, you know, and please, do try not to be incorrigible."

"That's it?"

I must have had a puzzled look on my face, because she nodded and said, "Honest! All you got to do is play along with him. If he says you're something or another, say, 'Oh yeah, that's it exactly.'"

"That's all?" I said.

She smiled again. "That's all."

So that's how I got to be there in Doctor Smiles's office, about to be swallowed up by a green leather chair, and telling myself to make sure to go along with whatever Doctor Smiles said about me.

He leaned back in his own chair so all I could see was the tip of his long thin nose with its black hair sticking straight out like bristles on a brush. His first words were, "Tell me about yourself."

I almost went into shock. I wanted to say, *You tell me and I'll agree,* but I decided that would be too obvious. Instead I said, "Tell me what you want me to tell you."

He suddenly sat straight up in his chair. When he spoke this time, I noticed he had a deep European accent and a high-pitched voice. "Are ve trying to argue?"

His *w*'s were pronounced like *v*'s, and he rolled his *r*'s. I wanted to say, *No ve aren't,* but I decided to do what Rebecca said and went along with it.

"If you say so, Doctor."

His eyes widened and he cocked his skinny head to the side so his jaw jutted out like the bottom of an upside-down question mark. "Say so vat?" he said.

"That we're arguing."

He leaned forward. "You are being capricious, right?"

I said, "Right," thinking that capricious was some kind of childhood disease.

He paused and I could see his eyes slowly become smaller. He reminded me of one of my cats about to pounce on something. "You are a most belligerent little girl," he said.

I said, "Yes, that too."

Suddenly his face seemed to turn a kind of orange-red, and he leaned forward across the desk and pointed his bony finger at me. "I can see you are going to be an evasive child with deep-seated emotional problems presenting themselves in chronic denial."

I almost jumped out of my chair—which was a mistake. When I came down, I sank even deeper. "That's it exactly, Doctor!"

It wasn't long before Doctor Smiles excused me. Whatever I said, it must have worked, because the next morning Mom came and picked me up. I wanted to thank Rebecca, but what I didn't know was, I owed it all to my mom. Later that day, I accidentally overheard her and my dad speaking on the telephone.

She said, "Doctor Ringleheim said she's a chronic paranoid schizophrenic who will require long-term psychotherapy and commitment for an indeterminate period of time."

I didn't exactly understand what she said, but it didn't sound good to me. There was a pause on the phone and I could hear Dad's voice, although I couldn't make out what he said. Whatever it was, it was loud. Mom stayed calm and said, "Don't get bent out of shape. I told Doctor Ringleheim he's crazier than she is!"

Just like Mom to compliment me like that.

The next thing she said didn't go over as well. "Yes, she is coming to you next weekend." Another pause. "I don't care how much she objects, she's not running the show. We are, and I'm not giving in to some made-up story about Juli's being Bloody Mary."

Uh oh, I thought, *I'm in for it now.* I was right. Except, it was worse than I thought.

13

Like Touching a Star

Dad remained quiet this trip. He wore his navy blue sweater and jeans. His heavy, green down coat lay across the back seat where I had tossed my backpack and school books. Ms. Breeze had assigned enough homework for the rest of the school year. I worked on my math while Dad drove. Every now and then I looked outside to see the snow that had covered the pastures overnight and now sparkled in the sunshine like a jillion tiny diamonds. Cars swooshed by us, making Dad shake his head and mumble comments about how someone ought to go back to driving school.

I wore my jeans and a sweater and was glad I brought along a short-sleeved shirt and shorts. Where Dad lives it's always warmer than my town. Before we left my house, he made me go back in and get my heavy coat. Dads are like that, always worrying about how their daughters dress. I was worried, too, but it wasn't about the weather.

Halfway to Dad's I finished my math. Well, maybe Ms. Breeze hadn't given enough homework to last the whole year after all. I smiled at Dad. I could tell he wanted to ask me about my therapy session with Doctor Smiles, but I knew he wouldn't unless I let him know it was okay. I said, "You'll never guess what I did last weekend."

He smiled. "Was it hard, honey?"

I nodded. "I was scared they'd keep me there."

"Your mom wouldn't let them do that," Dad said.

"Dad."

"What?"

"When you were a kid, did you believe in monsters?"

Dad cocked his head like he did when he was thinking. It looked like he wanted to be very careful about his answer, knowing what I'd been through with the psychiatrist and all. He took a deep breath and finally said, "Yes, I did."

"But you don't anymore, right?"

He didn't answer right away. He scratched his beard and looked up to the left. I figured that's where he kept his memories, because whenever he told me a story, he started out by looking up to his left. Now, he looked at me and smiled. "Amanda, there are lots of monsters in the world, even for grownups. Every time you go off on your own without me or your mom around, I'm afraid for you because of those monsters. But we've talked about them before."

I nodded. Dad had told me about grownups who kidnap children and do bad things to them, even kill them. "Dad, I know about those monsters. Honest I do. Those aren't the ones I mean. I mean the monsters with green eyes and long teeth and claws and...well, you know what I mean."

It was his turn to nod. "When I was a boy, my grandmother used to tell me if I wasn't good, the Boogeyman would come to take me away in a gunnysack. Most nights when I stayed over at her house to visit, I thought I could hear him walking past the bedroom."

I was sure I saw Dad shudder. "I was so scared," he said, "I couldn't sleep. So, you see, I did believe in monsters. But now, well...now I think you may have inherited my imagination."

"What do you mean, Dad?"

"I mean when I was your age, I could make up stories that really lived in my mind, but that's the only place they lived, except...."

"Except what, Dad?"

He shrugged his shoulders. "Nothing, honey. It's just my wild imagination, the same imagination you inherited."

"Dad, what's *inherited* mean?"

He laughed. "It's like you got your blue eyes from your mother and your skinny legs from your Aunt Polly, and from me you got the ability to make things up in your head."

"Yeah, but, Dad, Mom thinks I dreamed them, and the

shrink said I had some kind of pair of droids itchy frantic."

Dad laughed. "That's paranoid schizophrenic, which you don't have, but it tells me you listened in on your mom's conversation, and it also tells me you do have chronic nosiness."

"Daaaad!" I dropped my head and shrugged my shoulders.

Dad reached over and tossed my hair. He said, "Honey, you always were nosy. I suppose if your mom's going to talk on the phone, she's got to know you're going to try to listen in." I shrugged my shoulders again. "Anyway," he continued, "You're not paranoid schizophrenic. You're just like me, full of dreams and stories and always thinking you can reach up on a dark night and actually touch the stars."

I smiled. Dad knew me well. I did think I could touch the stars. But not only the stars. Sometimes I would go into my backyard, lie on the ground under a giant elm tree, and pretend I could touch the highest leaf. When I put my finger out I felt like I touched the leaf for real.

So we never got around to deciding if Dad believed me or not, or even if I believed myself. I admitted to myself that I had wonderful and sometimes totally terrifying dreams. I also knew I made up stories the other kids liked to hear. But I still couldn't decide if Juli had turned into Bloody Mary for real, or if it was all just a dream—or maybe a story I made up which then became real for me. Could I really reach up and touch a star at night or a leaf on the highest branch of a tree during the day?

14

Juli

She acted like nothing had happened. "Oh, Amanda, I missed you so." She welcomed me as soon as I got into the house from the garage. "Here, let me take your stuff for you. Mom made us some brownies. Oh, we're gonna have so much fun tonight. Guess who rented scary movies?"

She looked just like Juli—jeans, baggy sweatshirt, and baseball cap sideways on her head. She even smiled like Juli—braces gleaming, and her brown eyes twinkling when she told me about the movies. Even renting scary movies was one hundred percent Juli Kelley. I think she had watched *Jurassic Park* at least a hundred times. She had every line down to perfection. Sometimes, she would put it on the VCR when she was doing her homework, she told me once. But she always ran the risk her mom would come home early from work and bust her.

To be honest, I couldn't find anything about Juli that suggested Bloody Mary. By nine in the evening we had watched a movie about a monster who wore a hockey mask and used a chain saw to obliterate his enemies, and a really scary one about a high school girl who had the power to get even with kids who made fun of her. Juli said she especially liked that one.

"Want to play Barbies?" she said. It was our special secret, playing Barbies. We only played together because we were stepsisters and could trust each other. If our friends knew, we'd be ashamed. I often wondered if maybe my other friends didn't play secretly, too. Every now and then Juli's mom would come downstairs and play with us. She acted like she just wanted to be nice. You know, like spending quality time with us. But after a while I wondered if she didn't enjoy playing dolls as much as we did, the way her face lit up when she held them, and how good she was at making up situations for Barbie and Ken to get into.

Juli's mom had curly red hair and blue eyes and was from Houston, Texas. Every now and then she said things that sounded like the cowgirls on television. She only did that when she was playing with us, though. It was like she lost herself in the games and became Kay, the little girl, again. Last Christmas she bought her mom and my dad's mom sweatshirts that had a picture of a gray-haired lady on the front and read, "Grandmothers are just antique little girls."

I wondered if I would someday play Barbies with my own children. But right now, my interest was in playing with Juli.

"Sure! Let's play," I said.

Being older than me, Juli had every Barbie made, almost as many Kens, and Barbie clothes and toys, too. At least that's how it seemed to me. She kept them downstairs in the basement where we slept when I visited.

Before we went down there, Juli gave me a piece of information that made me feel much safer about playing in the basement. "Your Dad ran an extension cord downstairs so we can have a light on tonight," she said.

Dad, I love you, I thought to myself. *Now Juli won't be able to play her tricks on me again.* I was prepared this time. When I packed for the visit, I put a small flashlight in my backpack, a tiny crucifix I had received at my First Holy Communion, and a couple cloves of garlic taken from the kitchen where my mom kept her spices and stuff. Luckily I had the sense to put the garlic in a plastic bag. Still, I saw the way Juli and her mom sniffed the air and looked at my pack when Juli carried it in for me. If I wasn't careful, Kay would run it through the washer and the garlic would be ruined.

But now I felt relieved. I wouldn't have to worry about all that. Dad had taken care of me again. Besides, I had no way of knowing if that stuff would work against Bloody Mary. No problem. Now, with the new light and all, I felt I wouldn't have to worry.

Why is it, the minute you think everything is okay, it all seems to fall apart?

15

An Unwanted Invitation

It all started when Juli teased me about the last time I visited. "You're not still afraid I'm Bloody Mary?" she asked.

I said, "That's not funny, Juli."

She smiled at me over Ken's head, which she popped off and tossed in the air like a ball. Her voice lowered to a whisper. "Ever wonder what it feels like to have someone take your head off?"

"WHAT?" I was sorry as soon as I realized I had let her hear the fear in my voice.

She looked at me and her eyes seemed to widen. "Did I scare you, dearie?" She laughed. "Just kidding."

"Like the last time?" I said.

She smiled. Her face seemed genuine. "I'm sorry I scared you last time, Amanda. I was just playing. Really. I can do that you know."

"Do what?"

"Pretend to be someone I'm not. Want to see?"

"No!"

She laughed again. "You really are a little scaredy cat."

I was so embarrassed I could feel the blood rush into my face. I was sure she could see how flushed I must have been, so I tried to change the subject. "What are you getting for Christmas?"

She seemed to get serious and her eyes narrowed. "A new mirror. Someone broke the last one I played with."

I tried to ignore her.

She still tossed Ken's head up and down, and I was sure she did it to annoy me. "Are you coming to my Halloween party?"

She placed her face close to mine when she asked the question. Ever notice how different a person looks from really close? Juli definitely didn't look like herself. Kind of older or something.

That was enough for me. A tiny tear tried to work its way out of my eye, but I held it back. "You're being cruel, Juli. You've never treated me like this before, except...."

She smiled. "I'm sorry. Really, I mean it. Are you coming to my Halloween party?"

"Depends."

"On what?"

I couldn't tell her it depended on whether or not she was Bloody Mary, so I said, "On whether my mom lets me."

She stood up, put her hands on her hips, and said, "Oh that's easy. Follow me."

She ran up the stairs so fast I didn't have time to react. By the time I caught up with her, she was in the kitchen punching the buttons on the phone. I stood next to her, watching, wondering what she was up to this time. When the person on the other end of the line answered, Juli said, "Hello, Mrs. Terry. This is Juli Kelley. Amanda wants to ask you something."

She handed me the phone. My mouth was open wide enough to empty the trash into, but I managed to say, "Hi, Mom."

Juli stood right next to me, her ear almost as close to the receiver as mine. Mom said, "What's this all about? You two looking to get into more trouble?"

I hesitated, but Juli stared at me with an impatient look on her face and mouthed the words, *Ask her.* I still couldn't get the words out.

Mom said, "What is it, Amanda?" She sounded irritated now.

I still hesitated, feeling trapped. Finally Juli jerked the phone out of my hand and said, "Mrs. Terry, Amanda wants to came to my Halloween party. It's going to be at my house and we're going to stay at home instead of going trick or treating."

Juli hesitated, listening to what my mom had to say, then

she nodded and said, "Yes, it will be much safer than going out on those streets."

She hesitated again. A smile grew across her face. "Thank you," she said and hung up the phone. "You have your mother's permission. Wasn't that easy?"

I felt my face getting red, but this time it wasn't from embarrassment. "You could have let me ask her," I said. I wanted to say, *You could have let me make up my mind if I wanted to go or not.*

A dark feeling came over me, almost as bad as the one I experienced the last time I saw Juli. She wasn't herself. There was no doubt the real Juli would never have pushed me into doing something I didn't want to do.

Real friendship works like that. Sometimes when she and I had other things on our minds we didn't play together. But she never resented me when I was like that, and I respected her needs as well. It made for a great friendship. A couple of times my dad pointed it out to us.

"You girls are very special," he said. "Friendship means respecting each other's differences. The two of you are as different as night and day, yet you seem to love each other more because of it."

Dad had a way of showing us when we were doing something right. He let us know how important our friendship was. I wondered what he would think about Juli now. She didn't respect my feelings at all this time. She was being cruel to me, and I suspected it had something to do with last time I was there. I kept thinking that this wasn't the real Juli. *Maybe you're just dreaming this,* I said to myself.

I was totally confused. If I wasn't dreaming, it meant Juli really did turn into Bloody Mary.

Could it happen again?

16

Witch's Brew

The light Dad had rigged for us worked better than a flash-light. No batteries to run down. We played in the basement much later than usual. Juli wore one of her mother's old faded blue flannel nightgowns. I had on my pajamas, the ones with the red hearts my grandmother had given me for Valentine's Day. By the time we crawled into the sleeping bags, the clock on the wall said twelve-fifteen.

Juli was her old self again when we started playing. We giggled and laughed so hard my side hurt when I described how my ex-boyfriend Gerald Grandhopper dumped me:

"One day during recess, Gerald saw me playing with Jessica. Big mistake, according to Gerald. He said, 'I thought I told you not to talk to her anymore.'

"I told him, 'You got that one right, Charlie. Now try this one on for size. You don't have the right to tell me who I can or can't have for a friend. If you don't like it, we're not going out anymore.'"

"Cool!" Juli said. "Then what did he do?"

"His face got so red I thought it would explode, then he pushed me up against a fence. He raised his fist like he was about to hit me, and that's when I did something I probably shouldn't have done."

Juli's eyes got big and she said, "Did what?"

"I raised my hand and said, 'Go ahead, make my day.'"

Juli said, "What did he do, what did he do?"

"He screamed and ran across the yard yelling, 'Amanda Terry is going to hit me! Amanda Terry is going to hit me!'"

Juli laughed so hard I thought she would pass out. Her

face turned blue, she got tears in her eyes, and she kept saying, "Tell me again. What did he scream? Tell me again."

We talked about dumb boys—even some not so dumb—until very late. When we couldn't stop giggling, we knew it was time to sleep. I yawned and Juli couldn't keep her eyes open. She got out of her sleeping bag, went over to the corner of the room near the stairs, and reached for the extension cord to switch off the light.

"NO!" I screamed.

Juli turned to me with a puzzled look on her face.

I was so embarrassed. The word had come flying out of my mouth before I could stop it. She looked at me and cocked her head. I shrugged my shoulders. "I guess I just don't feel like sleeping in the dark tonight," I said.

She shrugged her shoulders and said, "Okay."

I was so relieved I must have fallen asleep the minute my head hit the pillow. But it wasn't long before something disturbed my sleep. I didn't open my eyes at first, but my nose was wide awake. Whatever woke me smelled totally awful. It was like someone had been cooking a dirty mop or maybe shoe leather, or…. Then I heard something move around in the corner, across the room from me. Whatever it was, it was breathing heavily, and I was sure I could hear a throat rattle, then a low, wicked sounding snicker.

"Not again," I whispered. "I must be dreaming." When I opened my eyes, the room was dark, and I could still hear the thing moving in the corner. "This can't be a dream," I whispered again.

A low, raspy voice began to sing a song in a language I couldn't understand. The melody was very low and monotonous, and sounded something like, "Splach, splich, flister, flick, eelga, oolga, blister, blick."

This went on for a while. Then it stopped, and the room got very quiet. Whoever was in the corner whispered something I did understand: "Almost time to add the main ingredient."

17

Bloody Mary

I could feel the goose bumps all over my body. Inside me everything turned cold. *This can't be happening again*, I tried to assure myself. *Bloody Mary is back, but how? Is Juli playing another cruel trick on me?* I wanted to laugh it off, but she cackled again, and my body started to shiver. I had to force my teeth to stop rattling so she wouldn't hear me.

I decided to run for it. She continued fussing around in the far corner, singing something I couldn't understand. The stairs ascended behind me. I could make it easily, if she didn't hear me.

Slowly, I slipped out of my sleeping bag. I agonized that she might hear me. She stopped moving, and I stayed still till I heard her humming to herself again. I could still smell whatever was cooking. Ugh! I wanted to gag. Almost out of the sleeping bag. Uh oh! My foot caught on a corner of the bag and made the zipper open a few inches. It wasn't much, but it was enough for her say, "What's that?"

I froze.

She drew in a deep breath and let it out. It sounded like a growl. Then she whispered to herself, "Soon, soon, be patient, soon my hunger will be satisfied."

I heard a sloshing sound, like she was stirring something in a kettle. She grunted with every movement. *Just like before*, I thought, *just like Bloody Mary*. Her breath, wheezing in and out, made me conscious of my own breathing. I tried to control it, taking in bits of air very slowly and exhaling just as carefully. She was still busy with her brew, but I wondered if she could sense that I was trying to escape.

Suddenly, she started singing again, that same low chant. More sloshing. She kept stirring whatever it was she had prepared for me.

I moved even slower, inching my way toward the stairs. My toe touched something—my backpack. I reached down and picked it up, carrying it in front of me like a baby doll. Finally, I reached the stairs and started up.

She stopped her chant, and I stayed still. "Just a tad more, almost ready for the main course," I heard her say.

Just a tad more, I said to myself. I was almost to the door at the top of the stairs when a thought crossed my mind.

"Wait a minute," I whispered just under my breath. "What if Juli's playing another one of her tricks on me, and I let her get away with it?"

Suddenly, there was a burning in my chest. She's being cruel again. She wants me to run screaming to my dad. She wants him to believe I'm just dreaming. "Juli," I whispered, "I can't believe you'd think you could make a fool out of me again."

That's when I turned around and slipped quietly back down the stairs. *My flashlight—it's in my pack.* I reached in and found it on the top where I'd placed it, just in case. *This time, the trick is on you, Juli.*

I descended to the bottom of the stairs, then tiptoed closer to the sound of the weird chant Juli had made up to convince me she was Bloody Mary.

"Ick, wick, bick, tick," she said. With every word, I put one foot ahead of the other until I stood just a few feet away. I had the flashlight ready. "Whoosh, coosh, boosh, doosh," she sang, to which I answered in a loud confident voice:

"Roses are red, violets are blue, flashlight in your face, the trick is on you!"

I turned on the light, pointed it straight at her, and said, "You won't fool me ever again."

She didn't jump like I thought she would. She was facing away from me, still wearing that old blue flannel nightgown, but her head was bent over, and her hands were occupied so I couldn't see what she was doing.

"Turn around, Juli," I said, "so I can see what stuffed animal you've got in your hands this time."

She cackled and I felt a shiver down my back. She did a great imitation of Bloody Mary, I would give her that.

But I held my ground. "Won't work this time, DEARIE. I know what you want me to do. You want to make me run screaming to my dad like the last time. Well, it won't work, so you may as well turn around and forget about scaring me."

"Very well," I heard her say. She made her voice deep and raspy like she had before when she scared me for real. "I was ready to eat you, anyway. Now I won't have to chase you," she said.

"Yeah, sure," I said, "You'll nibble my nose and gobble my ears."

She started to turn slowly and said, "Why, no, dearie. That's not exactly what I plan to do. I'm going to gobble your nose and nibble on your ears."

She was finally turned all the way around and I held the flashlight straight at her. But something was wrong.

Her hair covered her face. No, wait. It wasn't Juli's hair. It was long and black with strands of gray.

I laughed and reached over to pull it away from her. "That old wig won't work either, Juli." When I touched it, my hand jerked back instinctively. *Oh yuck*, I thought. It felt oily, slick like the slime I felt in the garbage can when I retrieved the box that held the mirror.

Suddenly I went cold again inside. I didn't reach for her hair again. I didn't have to.

She said, "You want to see my face, don't you, dearie?"

My mouth couldn't have answered if it had wanted to. It was frozen open, just as my hand was frozen with the flashlight splashing its yellow light on the person I no longer believed was Juli who was playing a trick on me.

The hands came up from her side. I saw hair on her arms, thick black curly hair, thick as the fur of animals. Her hands were twisted, and the fingernails were long and gnarled and dirty. She reached in front of herself and parted her greasy hair with those fingernails.

If I could have screamed, I would have. It was Bloody Mary, not the warm, beautiful Juli who was my loving stepsister. It was the monster I saw in the mirror when I first looked into the box. Her mouth parted into a crooked smile, and the teeth flashed against the light. She took a deep breath and let it come out in a low growl. Then she spoke. "Hello, sister. Ready for supper. I'm sooo hungry. I haven't eaten in a hundred years. I'll gobble your nose and nibble on your ears."

Suddenly, she sprang out at me, and I fell backwards, the flashlight in my hand streaking back and forth around the room. I was on my back, trying to crawl backwards, all the time watching her shuffle toward me with those wicked hands grasping out to take hold of me. "Don't run," she said. "You're only putting it off."

I reached the stairs, managed to turn on my stomach, and began to crawl up the steps like a baby. All the time my flashlight was bouncing around the room. Time seemed to go into slow motion. I could even count the stair steps as I crawled up toward the door. One, two, three, four, five....

At five she hooked one of her crooked fingernails in the seat of my pajamas. I heard her laugh and say, "Yes! Now, I have you!"

My voice finally came back to me, and I screamed, "Eat pajamas, you old witch," as I slipped out of the bottoms and reached the door. I was mortified to find myself standing at the top of the stairs wearing my Huggy Bear panties. But when I stepped out and slammed the door behind me, I decided it was much better to be an embarrassment than a meal.

That's when I screamed, *"HELP"* just loud enough for the entire neighborhood to hear me.

18

Not Again

Dad didn't even bother to ask me what was wrong.

I waited at the top of the stairs.

When he came up from the basement, he had an ugly rubber mask in one hand. He held it up. The face of a wicked looking, wrinkled witch with long black hair stared at me. In his other hand Dad carried my pajama bottoms. He smiled. "I found this mask on a chair in the corner and your pajamas hooked on a nail halfway up the stairs. He handed me the bottoms. "Put them on, now," he said as he laughed. "Aren't you a little old for Huggy Bears?"

"But Dad, what about the witch's brew?"

"Yes," he said, "the witch's brew. I think if you look downstairs in the corner where I found this mask, you'll see Juli's terrible-smelling science project. Not exactly perfume, honey. But certainly not lizard tails and toad eyes. Now, why don't you go down with me so I can show you Juli, still asleep in her sleeping bag?"

I shook my head. This time I couldn't keep the tears from sneaking out of my eyes. "I'm not going down there, Dad. I don't care if you think I had a bad dream or not. I'm not sleeping down there ever again."

In the morning, all was normal. Juli ate a breakfast of waffles and bacon, while I ate cereal. She kept smiling at me from across the table. I wanted to say something, but I decided the less I said the better. She even hugged me when we left. "Don't forget my Halloween party," she said. This time she didn't follow it up with *dearie*.

Dad could see I was disturbed. We had driven halfway to

Mom's house and I hadn't said anything to him. He took my hand and said, "What's happened to my chatterbox little girl?"

I shrugged my shoulders.

Dad didn't let it go. "Honey, I'm really lost about what to do. Your dreams are getting much worse, and...."

"Tell me more," I said.

"What?" Dad had a surprised look on his face.

"You know," I said, "the monster you saw when you were a little boy."

"Hmmm," he said, then pursed his lips and let go of my hand so he could scratch the side of his beard. Then he smiled at me, took my hand back, and said, "Why not?"

I was excited because Dad was a writer, and when he told a story, he told it like it was happening now. When I was younger, he would tell me stories before I fell asleep at night. He would ask me what kind of story I wanted to hear, then make one up just for me. Most of the time I wanted scary stories, but if they got too scary, I would stop him and ask him to make up a happy ending so I wouldn't have bad dreams. Funny, looking back, I almost never had a bad dream when Dad told me his bedtime stories. This time, I was sure his story would be scary. I knew because it would be the story of his very own personal monster.

He looked at his watch. "Okay, Amanda. We have time. Why don't you lay the seat back and pretend it's bedtime?"

I just loved that. Dad always knew how to play pretend. I reached into the back seat and found my jacket. It felt like a blanket when I pulled it over my legs and up under my arms.

I closed my eyes and Dad started his story. His voice was low and serious sounding, and he said something that surprised me: "No one in my entire life ever scared me like my grandmother did." His voice changed back to normal. "Of course, she loved me too. And I loved her. She was my very first storyteller. But she was more than that. Before I was full-grown, I was sure Grandma was a witch."

19

The Boogeyman

"Every day, after school," Dad said, "I would race home, change into my play clothes, and run the half-mile to Grandma's house for story time. She would sit me down in the story rocker, a yellow metal patio rocker she kept right there in her bedroom where she sat on the bed and told stories.

"Before the stories began, she would send me to the kitchen for a jelly roll and an RC Cola, my story time snack. Then she started telling. She could talk about anything. She was a large woman, your great-grandmother was. Large round arms and legs, big as tree trunks. Her body looked like a well-fed gnome. Some people would call her fat. She never used that word, though. She said she was stout.

"On top of her body rested a proud head with long auburn hair she kept rolled up and placed in a bun. Every now and then, I would watch her make herself beautiful.

"In the morning before breakfast, she sat at her vanity and put her makeup on. Her hair was long and wavy—it reached way past her bottom and looked as flashy as a horse's mane. I can still see her brown eyes sparkle. She always held her head up straight so her nose seemed higher than it should have been. I loved to watch her sit at her dresser and slap powder on her face with a powder puff as fat as a pancake. And her stories!" A big smile spread across Dad's face.

"Her stories sometimes kept me sitting in that old metal rocker till it got past dark and I had to run home to do my homework. She told me about her life on the ranch. She was a cowgirl, you see. Her daddy, who looked something like Robert E. Lee, owned a large cattle ranch down in Texas. He fought in the War Between the States. Grandma told stories about that too, and about slavery, and the cruel things people could do to one another."

Dad took a deep breath and sighed. I felt his hand squeeze mine a little harder. "That was the good, loving part of my grandma. Then there were the stories of the monster. You still want to hear about the monster, don't you?"

I didn't have to open my eyes to say, "Uh huh."

"Okay," Dad said. His voice got serious again. "Sometimes, because my mother and father were poor, they had to leave me with my grandma for a while. Grandma was different when I stayed with her. She had rules, and if I broke them, she had old-fashioned ways of punishing me. First, she used a switch. You do know what a switch is, don't you?"

I shrugged my shoulders. "I'm not sure."

"A switch is a small limb from a tree or bush. Grandma used it to spank me, or as she used to say, to switch me. It stung, but it never did any serious damage. So, you see, I got used to the switch, and she had to resort to the monster."

I felt Dad's hand tighten a little more when he said *monster*. He continued his story:

"To understand the monster, you have to know what Grandma's house looked like. It was down at the edge of town, in a neighborhood where most of the houses were fallen down or abandoned. Just walking down there at night was a scare. You had to pass an abandoned graveyard. We kids knew that the dead who rested there didn't like being taken for granted. Remember when I said I would run home from grandma's house when it got dark?"

I said, "Yes."

"It was because of the graveyard. During the day, it looked like any old cemetery with broken granite tombstones and iron crosses and fences surrounded by weeds and scraggly hackberry trees. But at night, the wind whistled through those trees and moved the limbs around so they looked like creatures howling at the moon and pleading for someone to keep them company.

"You can imagine how it felt to sleep at Grandma's house. From my bedroom window, I could see into the cemetery.

Worse than that was the house itself. You're not going to believe this, but I swear it's true. The house was bigger inside than outside. Outside, it was a tiny, unpainted, dark shack sitting under towering pecan trees, situated down a dark lane fifty yards or so off a dirt road. Sometimes, even in the day, the trees kept the light out, so I felt like I was walking into a cave when I went to hear Grandma's stories. But at night...." Dad shuddered.

"At night, it was dark and damp as a tomb. At least, that's how I remember it. Grandma didn't have electricity, so she used oil lamps. The flames would flicker and cast ghostly shadows. Worst part of all, my bedroom was in the back of the house, and Grandma's was in front. When I went back there at night carrying an old oil lamp, it was like I was entering a corridor into a dungeon. That's what I meant when I said it was bigger inside than outside.

"I swear, if you looked at the house from the outside, you would guess it had one, maybe two rooms. But when you went inside, it seemed to go on forever. On one side of the house was Grandma's bedroom, which was really the parlor. She put her bed in there so she could sit on it to tell stories or lie down to sleep when she felt like it. Behind her room was a dark dining room and then a kitchen that seemed twice as tall as the other two rooms. In the kitchen was the oak icebox where grandma kept her RC Colas, some milk, eggs, butter, and not much else.

"Everywhere I looked in that old kitchen there were shelves and cabinets that seemed too tall for a regular human being to reach. It felt like the walls were twenty feet high. They were covered with dark wooden shelves full of jars, bowls, and strange-looking dried weeds. I never knew what they were. But if you asked me today, I would say they might be the ingredients for magic spells and potions.

"Off to one side was a free-standing cupboard with a flour mill where she kept real flour she sifted to make bread. The stove was black and massive—a coal cooker with glittering stainless steel trim and an oven big enough to bake.... To be honest, I always called it the Hansel and Gretel oven because it was big enough to bake a kid in."

Wow! I thought. I couldn't imagine a stove that big. I wanted to ask Dad what she baked in that oven, but I also wanted him to get to the part about the monster. The story intrigued me enough to sit up and open my eyes. I kept real quiet and listened as he described the most unbelievable part about the house.

"On the other side of the house," Dad said, "were the bedrooms." He shivered again. "I guess they were bedrooms. I was allowed to look inside only one, the room where I slept. It was located at the very back of the house."

He looked at me, and his hazel eyes suddenly seemed very large. "You're not going to believe this, Amanda, but it seemed like I passed five doors on either side of the dark hallway before I got to my own room."

"Gaaaaaahhh!" I couldn't help myself. "Gaaah, Dad," I said again, "weren't you scared?"

He shrugged his shoulders. "Not at first. When I was smaller, I just figured that was the way all grandmothers' houses looked. It was only after she told me about the monster that I started wondering."

"Wondering what, Dad?"

"Wondering about my grandmother. Do you still want to hear the part about the monster?"

I nodded.

"Okay," Dad said, turning his head to the side so his eyes could look up to the left where he kept his memories. "Time came when I thought I was too big to pay attention to Grandma's rules. The time I brought a six-foot bull snake into the house was the last time I tested her. That's when she told me about the Boogeyman."

"Oh, is that all?" I said. "Daaaad, that's just an old kids' story."

Dad looked at me with eyes that didn't smile. "That's what I used to think. But that night, I learned better. That night was the first night I heard him." Dad's voice got very low and I had to lean closer to him to hear.

"It was past midnight, and I was breaking another of Grandma's rules by reading under the covers with a flashlight. I was reading this library book about a little girl who had turned into a glob of killer tar when I heard something outside my window—the window that opened out toward the graveyard. It was a scratchy noise. At first, I thought a shutter had broken loose and was scraping against the side of the house. After a few moments, it didn't sound like that, but more like the kind of scraping something makes when it's being dragged across the ground. I immediately thought of Grandma's warning that the Boogeyman puts bad kids in gunnysacks and drags them to his hideaway where he eats them.

"I could see the Boogeyman in my mind even though I kept telling myself it was all a scary kids' story. I could still hear the scratching, and in my imagination I saw an ugly bent-over man with a dark overcoat and large hat pulled down over his eyes pulling along a brown gunnysack full of children."

Dad's story was so scary that I could see the Boogeyman, too. I could see Dad's monster in my own mind. He was tall and had on a dirty brown wool overcoat with a ragged hem and missing buttons. He wore a large hat pulled low so his eyes were hidden and his large hands poked out of the sleeves of his coat—hands big enough to pick up a kid by the neck and squash him into the gritty gunnysack he carried with him.

My eyes were wide open, looking at Dad's eyes which were twice as wide as mine. "Really, Dad, did you really see him?"

He shook his head. "Not that time. That time I huddled under the covers and prayed I was just imagining things. Next morning though, Grandma told me no kid can hide under covers from...the Boogeyman."

He smiled. "I obeyed Grandma's rules from then on."

I let out a big sigh. "Bet you did. So that was it, huh? That's the story of your monster?"

Dad's smile faded just a little. I didn't miss it and said, "There's more, huh?"

"Yes, there's more. From that time on, I could hear him every time I visited Grandma's. When I got braver, I would wait for him to pass by the house, then I'd creep slowly out of bed, tiptoe over to the window, and pull the shade up a tad to try to see him."

"Did you, Dad? Did you see him?"

Dad took a really deep breath and let it out slowly. "Well, I would suppose you could say...well, I thought it was my imagination. I would look over to the graveyard, into a dark stand of mangled hackberry trees. I used to imagine I could see him there. You know, like pretend?"

I nodded. If anyone could play pretend it was me.

"Then," Dad continued, "the last time I ever visited my grandmother, I had an experience that made me wonder."

Dad's face lost some of its color. His eyes narrowed and he spoke very softly. "I was older then, about your age. I'd gotten used to pretending I could see the Boogeyman, and I guess I wasn't so afraid of him anymore. Anyway, I waited for him to pass by one night. By that time, I was convinced a dog or cat or some small animal was actually making the noise that I used to think was the Boogeyman. Still I waited to hear the noise. But I didn't. That night there was no sound of something being dragged by the house. I slipped out of my bed and looked anyway. I pulled up the shade, cupped my hands to my face so I could see through the window, and looked off into the hackberry stand. Nothing."

"Nothing," I whispered almost as low as Dad was speaking.

"Nothing," he said, "except...."

"Except what, Dad?"

"Except I had a sensation that made the hairs on the back of my neck stand straight up and every goose bump in my body come to attention."

"What kind of sensation?" I asked.

"The kind of sensation you get when you sense that someone's spying on you."

I took a deep breath and held it. I didn't want to hear the rest of Dad's story but I knew I had to. "Go on," I said.

Dad looked at me. "You sure?"

"Yes."

"Okay, picture this: I'm standing there at the window, shades drawn halfway up, looking out into the graveyard. Suddenly, I feel someone is very close, close enough I can smell him, close enough I feel I can reach out and touch him.

Very slowly, I turn to the right, so slowly, I feel almost paralyzed. And suddenly, I want to scream and jump out of my skin and run, but I can't. I can't because I know he hasn't seen me yet."

Now I wanted scream. "Who hasn't seen you yet?"

"A very large man dressed in a brown overcoat with a hat drawn low over his eyes. He has two enormous hands cupped to his face, and he's looking straight into my bedroom on the other side of the same window I'm looking out from."

Dad's story made me cold all over. I wanted to say something but I couldn't. All I could do was stare at Dad with my mouth open. Finally, I said, "Then what?"

Dad looked at me and said, "I knew he hadn't seen me yet because he was looking at the bed behind me, off to my right. So I froze and waited, hoping he would give up and go away. It seemed like forever. I thought he could hear my breath for sure. My heart pounded so loud I was afraid it would explode and I would die of fright. Then, as suddenly as he appeared, he was gone. Poof, just like that."

I said, "Then what happened, Dad?"

Dad's voice was so low I could barely make it out. "Very carefully, I pulled down the shade and crept back to my bed, pulled the cover up, and stayed as quiet as I could. That's when it happened."

"What, Dad?"

"I heard the dragging again. Outside, the wind howled like all the ghosts in the graveyard had come out to play. But I could still hear the dragging. That's when I knew."

"Knew what?" I said.

Dad said, "That's when I knew he had come to get me. I was as sure of that as I was of anything. He had come for me, and I was saved only because he couldn't see me in the bed."

It was real quiet in the car for a long time. Dad kept his head straight ahead and drove like it was all he had to do for the rest of his life. Finally I had to ask, "Do you still believe you saw the monster, Dad?"

He reached over and put his hand on mine. "I don't know, honey. It's been so long, I don't know what I remembered or what I made up. I know one thing, though. You have the same kind of imagination I have, and it's going to give you all kinds of monsters in the dark at night." He smiled. "I do know this, too, Amanda—I love you."

I closed my eyes and fell asleep holding my daddy's hand. In my dreams I saw the Boogeyman and Dad having a fight. Dad won, of course. Then I saw Bloody Mary. She was standing right next to me, watching the dream. When I looked over, she spoke, "Your dad never had to face ME. No one will ever get away from me. That includes you, dearie."

20

Confused

Can kids get confused? My mom thinks I'm disturbed, so she sends me to Doctor Smiles. He thinks I'm crazy, but Mom saves me from him because she knows I'm not. Still, Mom doesn't believe Bloody Mary is more than a bad dream. Dad, on the other hand, believes in monsters but doesn't believe I'm seeing one. Not really. Then on the other hand...I give up.

When Mom asked, "How did it go at your dad's?" I said okay. No use pushing for another visit to the shrink.

Things weren't okay. I couldn't sleep at night. No appetite. Not that unusual except I was going through a growth spurt and I usually eat like a garbage disposal when I go through a growth spurt.

The first to notice was Ms. Breeze, but not before Jessica suspected something. Recess was half over, and I decided to go back to the classroom.

Jessica looked at me and shook her head.

"I just don't feel like playing today," I said.

She must have taken it personally. I could tell she was frustrated with me since I hadn't been much of a friend for several days.

"Suit yourself," she said, then she ran back to the playground, leaving me to feel sorry for myself.

Halfway down the hall to my classroom, I heard music, rock music. It was coming from my room. *Very strange*, I thought. You know how you suppose teachers make use of every free moment to sit in the classroom and grade papers? I discovered that isn't all they do. At least not all Ms. Breeze does. When I reached the door to my classroom, the music stopped. Good. *Now I won't embarrass her*, I thought. But soon as I stepped in, another song started:

"Jeremiah was a bullfrog.

"Was a good friend of mine...."

Ms. Breeze was a sight. Her purple cotton granny dress whirled up past her knees, so I had a clear shot at her black combat boots and gray wool socks with red trim. She had her hair in a ponytail, and she wasn't wearing her granny glasses just then. The wooden bracelets she wore rattled as they bounced up and down her arm. I never saw a teacher dance before, not like that anyway.

As soon as she saw me she froze. Then she slowly reached over and pushed the stop button on the cassette player. We looked at each other for a second or two then broke out laughing at the same time.

"You caught me doing aerobics," she said, trying to catch her breath.

"Sure," I said.

We laughed again. If that was aerobics, it was the funkiest aerobics I'd ever seen.

She said, "Amanda, this is the first time all week I've seen you look like yourself. Want to tell me what's wrong?"

I shrugged my shoulders and said, "Nothing."

"Look," she said, "you've never cut recess short as long as I've known you. Even when you're sick, you find a way to play. You haven't been paying attention in class, which isn't unusual. What is unusual is that you haven't even tried to pass notes to Jessica or Josie either." I smiled. "Gotcha," she said. "Now why don't we have a girl to girl talk?"

She led me over to the snack table where kids were allowed treats for obeying the rules. It was one of the few times I'd been there. Ms. Breeze was strict and had lots of rules, but she never made me feel I was bad for not always following them. Instead she put me on her work crew. Work crew students were like the opposite of snack table students. She always praised me for the good work I did for her.

Every now and then, she would explain why her rules were so important, and I would try hard to obey them. But she had to remind me more often than the other students. This time was different. She seemed to know my problem had nothing to do with school.

"Try this." She handed me a chocolate cupcake. She cut herself a slice of the homemade bread she would bring to school sometimes. It smelled better than the chocolate. Better than chocolate? Now I knew something was wrong.

She looked at the clock over her desk. "We have ten minutes. Let's talk."

I took a deep breath, then opened my mouth. Nothing came out. All of a sudden, I felt a hurt in my chest. I tried to keep the tears back but couldn't. Ms. Breeze reached over and touched my hand. That's all it took. Pretty soon, she had her arms around me, and I was crying like a baby. Funny thing is, I didn't even feel bad about it. The bell rang, and she told me to go to the bathroom and said I didn't have to come back until I felt okay about returning to class. "I still want to talk," she said. "Let's try after school. Your mother won't mind. Heaven knows I've had to keep you after school often enough as it is."

21

Girl Talk

Riiiiinnnggggg!

Ms. Breeze yelled, "Walk, don't run!"

It didn't matter. For some reason the last school bell of the day always sounds the loudest. Or is it because we're all listening the closest for it? She tried again. "Slow down, you'll live longer."

But we all knew better. Living was after school.

All of a sudden the classroom became quiet. Eventually the buzz of the kids talking and yelling outside faded as well. For some reason I shuddered. I always thought an empty school felt eerie. Ms. Breeze read my mind. "I hate empty classrooms," she said.

She remained behind her desk, pencil in hand, brown eyes focused on a paper she was grading. "I'll be right with you, Amanda."

I moved my chair, and the legs squeaked and echoed. I wanted to yell, *Hello,* to see if my voice would bounce around the room. If I had been alone, I would have done that. Outside, all the kids had run to the front where the buses and their parents waited, so I could hear birds chirping and squirrels chattering. Usually, that would have cheered me up, but my chest still felt heavy, and I had to tell myself not to cry again. I watched Ms. Breeze look up from the paper and smile.

She folded whatever it was she had on her desk and put it neatly to one side. "Let's walk outside," she said. "We can talk there. The sun's shining and I don't want to miss it."

She was right about the sun. It did feel good. I couldn't

get enough of my body inside my coat when I walked to school in the morning. Now my bare arms felt tingly in the heat.

We walked across the playground to the merry-go-round.

"You push me first," she said, "then I'll push you."

We wound up sitting next to each other, holding on and watching the whole world go around.

"Want to tell me what's on your mind?" she asked.

"Promise you won't laugh at me?"

"Not unless it's funny. Sometimes I can't help myself, Amanda. If something strikes me as funny, I break out. Know what I mean?"

I nodded. "I do that myself sometimes. But I don't see anything funny about what I'm feeling just now. I try to tell myself I'm only dreaming. Mom thinks that's all it is, and Dad confuses me."

Ms. Breeze turned toward me and cocked her head to the side. Her bangs blew across her eyes. "Is this about monsters, Amanda?"

I nodded.

"Wow!" she said. "It's great to hear I'm not the only one who still believes in monsters."

I thought she was humoring me so I said, "I'm serious."

"So am I, Amanda, so am I." She looked serious too.

That's when I told her about the mirror, my dreams, how Mom thought I was crazy and Dad didn't know what to make of me, and most of all about Bloody Mary. When I finished, I waited for her to give me advice or maybe tell me to see the school nurse. She didn't. Instead she said, "Well, what do you think you should do about it?"

It was my turn to cock my head to the side. "Do about what?"

"Everything," she said, "about everything that's been happening to you."

I guess she could hear the exasperation in my voice when I said, "I've tried everyone. There's no one who can help me. I feel so alone I could...."

She cut me off and said, "What about yourself, Amanda? Have you tried solving the mystery yourself?"

That's when it hit me. *Cool! I guess there are times when*

a girl has to solve her own problems.

When I said so to Ms. Breeze, she nodded. "That's right, Amanda. I really wish it weren't that way, but there are times when we all have to solve our own problems without help." She must have seen the hopeless look on my face, because she continued, "It's what growing up is all about. Moms and dads are the best things in the world for us, but there comes a time when we have to rely on ourselves."

"Ms. Breeze?"

She smiled. "Yes, Amanda?"

"Don't you think I'm a little young to be solving my own problems?"

She took a deep breath and said, "Well, I would say yes if your parents seemed to want to help. But it looks like they're out of it when it comes to solving monster problems. Grownups don't do well in the monster category." She brushed her bangs out of her face again. "Most grownups are too old to believe kids really see the kinds of things they also used to see when they were kids. Later on, when parents are older and not so bothered by trying to make a living and pay for food and rent and clothes, they become more interested in monster problems again."

"How about you, Ms. Breeze?" I looked up at her with my most pleeeeaaasse-help-me look on my face. "Can't you help me?"

She reached out and touched my hand. "I just did help you, Amanda. I believed you."

I smiled back at her. "Yes, you did," I said. "And I felt really warm inside when you did."

The merry-go-round stopped, and we got off and started to walk back toward the school.

Ms. Breeze said, "Tell you what I'll do. I'll be available to listen to you any time you want to talk about the monster. But you must find your own way out of the predicament you're in. Grownup solutions don't usually work with monsters because grownups don't believe in tried-and-tested monster solutions."

I said, "Like changing the spell by saying "Bloody Mary" into the mirror in the dark?"

"That's exactly it, Amanda. Grownups believe in logical, scientific solutions, not magic mirrors and haunted houses and spells."

I took a deep breath and suddenly felt a burst of energy running through my body. It was as if I had struggled to reach the highest part of a roller coaster and was just about to fly downhill. I only hoped I'd be able to put on the brakes before I crashed.

22

Detective Amanda

It was Saturday. I stood in the library.

Me in a library?

The only other times I had gone there was when the whole class went. But that was always for an assignment, and I usually got busted for talking to Jessica. This time it was different. This time I went on my own—to do detective work.

First, I typed the words *Bloody Mary* into the computer. Not much came up except a few references to a queen in Scotland and a short story in *Bruce Coville's Book of Monsters.*

I found that book in the juvenile section and read the story as fast as I could. Scary. Kind of like what happened to me. Well, at least I wasn't the only girl who claims she was almost eaten by Bloody Mary. In the story, the mirror worked only one way. The wrong way. I mean, the girl who said the words became Bloody Mary. But the spell didn't really reverse itself when the words were said in the mirror in the dark. I was right back where I started.

A part of me wanted to give up. I even considered what excuse I could make up to avoid going to my Dad's next week. Halfway out of the library, it hit me that I really should try some of the other reference books about the other Bloody Mary, the one who was a queen.

Gosh, European history books are heavy. The references were about Mary, Queen of Scots, who was certainly bloody but had nothing to do with mirrors. I was almost ready to give up when a sentence in a footnote said something that caught my attention. It was way down at the bottom of the page in very small print. I sounded it out to make sure it said what I thought it said:

> Legend has it that the ghost of Mary, Queen
> of Scots, wanders the world, haunting the
> reflections of evil women.

You should have seen the goose bumps pop up all over my body.

"Reflections?" I whispered. "Like reflections in a mirror?"

I went back upstairs where the biography books were stacked and began to look for anything about Mary, Queen of Scots. Nothing. Then it occurred to me to look for books on Scotland. I found half a dozen. I was on a roll. Everyone had chapters on Queen Mary. I read four. No reference to the legend that Mary haunted reflections of evil women. By the fifth book, I decided I had probably wasted time, except I had to admit I was fast becoming somewhat of an expert on Queen Mary. That's when I came to a section of one book all about Queen Mary's jewelry.

You should have seen my eyes bug out. There in living color was a painting of a collection of jewelry including two jeweled mirrors that looked like copies of the one I had discovered in my attic. The same mirror I had broken in the basement of Juli's house. There was nothing about the curse. I read the rest of the books and found nothing there.

Not much to go on, I thought. *Except...two mirrors—not one—but two mirrors.* And, of course, the mystery only seemed to grow. I wondered if the mirror I found in the attic and the ones shown in the painting were from the same set? And if so, how did it come to be in my house?

I had to go on. It was still a puzzle, and maybe even a bigger one than I had previously thought, but some of the pieces seemed to fit.

Okay, Amanda, I told myself, *you can't quit now.* So I went up to the librarian who got this strange look in her dark eyes when I said, "I'm looking for a book on Queen Mary's jewelry."

"Honey," she said, "Why don't you let me show you how to use the computer reference system."

I gulped.

Piece of cake! It took her less than five minutes to teach me how to punch in the information for my search. Surprise! Three books on European jewelry were in the library. Not one of them had ever been checked out. I found them in the stacks and took them to a table downstairs. By the third book I was becoming a whiz at reading indexes. Finally, a section on Celtic jewelry, and there it was, the same painting of Queen Mary's jewelry, including the mirrors. This time, there was a caption under the photograph of the painting, telling me where I could find the jewels displayed in the Tower of London. I did a double take when the caption went on to explain that some of the original jewels were missing. A few items had been stolen and were rumored to have been taken to the Americas by exiled Scots who remained loyal to Mary.

"Yes!"

The librarian's dark eyes glared at me.

This time I whispered, "Yes."

I deduced that I might find out more about the mirrors if I could drag up information on the people who had lived in our house. It occurred to me that I might be a natural detective the way I was deducing and all. I already knew there was a ghost haunting the place. Now, I had to learn about the house where I lived and the ghost who lived with me. Could it be Queen Mary herself? Or maybe a descendant of one of Mary's loyal followers who had possession of the mirror I had discovered?

As the mystery grew, so did the questions. Not the least of which was, if there really was a spell on the mirror, how could I reverse it? I had heard that you could reverse the spell by having the monster say "Bloody Mary" in the mirror, in the dark. *Well, that didn't work,* I said to myself. *Amanda, you have got find out more about the haunted house where you live.*

That night, as I lay in my bed trying to figure out what to do next, I heard a noise in the hallway outside my room. Someone walking softly, like Mom does when she doesn't want to disturb me. Suddenly I needed a hug. I really needed one, so I slipped out of my bed, went over to the door, and opened it announcing, "Mommy, I think this is a mother-daughter moment."

The steps in the hallway ceased, and I waited. I smelled the scent of lilacs again and knew for sure that it wasn't my mother passing by outside my room. "Never mind," I whispered, surprised how firm my voice sounded. That's when I knew for sure there was a ghost in my house, and it was trying to tell me something I really needed to know.

23

A Trip to the Past

Saturday morning, I ate an early breakfast and walked to the town museum. I remembered an exhibit of old books and pictures about the original homes and families who founded the city.

Ours was not an ordinary museum, where the artifacts are inside a big building and you have to stand behind ropes or other barriers to see the exhibits. Our museum has two real farms on the grounds, one from the early nineteen hundreds and another farm from the middle eighteen hundreds. You can go inside the houses and see people pretending they really lived during those time. You can even watch live farm animals and see how the gardens grow.

Smells like a farm, too. Fresh cut hay and straw, smoldering coals from the blacksmith shop, and the—ugh—odor of the pigs in their sties. But it wasn't the animals that interested me. The last time I visited, I saw a wonderful collection of photographs of all the original houses in our town. The exhibit had been held in the farmhouse from the early nineteen hundreds.

The farmhouse has two bedrooms, a parlor, dining room, and kitchen added on later. The ceilings are tall and the windows as big as doors. It reminds me of a dollhouse my grandfather made for me. But the dollhouse has a bathroom. The real one doesn't. An outhouse stands out back, closer to the barn.

I was disappointed.

The exhibit had been in the parlor, but it was no longer there.

Maybe in another room, I thought. No luck. All five rooms had been furnished the way they were in the early nineteen hundreds. But no pictures of old houses. I sat down on the Victorian sofa in the parlor, put my elbows on my knees and my head in my hands, and gave out a big sigh of disappointment.

That's when I heard the voice from the bedroom: "Honey, fetch me a tumbler of water."

24

The Storyteller Appears

She must have come in after I went through the house, because I was positive there had been no one in the house but me. At first, I wasn't sure she was talking to me. But she spoke again, this time louder. "In the icebox, young lady. Big pitcher of cold water in the icebox. There's a soda there for you. Look on the woodstove. Find you a jelly roll, nice and warm, to snack on whilst I tell you a story."

I still couldn't see her from where I sat, but I went back to the kitchen and found the oak icebox. You should have seen the surprise in my eyes when I opened it and saw the water and one bottle of RC Cola. I'd never heard of RC Cola until my dad told me about how his grandmother used to tell him stories while he drank an RC Cola and snacked on a...the word *jelly roll* didn't want to come out of my mouth. But it was there, just where she said it would be, a jelly roll, warm and inviting on top of the woodstove.

"It's your imagination, Amanda," I whispered to myself. "Must be a storyteller hired by the museum to pretend she lives in the house."

I tried not to think about the coincidence with Dad and his grandma who served him an RC Cola and jelly roll when she told him stories.

I poured a large glass of water and juggled that with my soda and snack all the way back through the parlor and into the bedroom. When I stepped inside the room, I almost dropped everything.

Sitting there on the side of the bed was an older woman, her small head posed on her shoulders, auburn hair put up in a bun, and arms and legs big as tree trunks. She could have been the very image of how my daddy described his grandmother. My mouth opened even wider when I saw a yellow metal patio rocker sitting across from the bed. Daddy did say his grandmother had him sit in a yellow metal patio chair when she told him stories. The word *eerie* came to my mind.

"That there's the story chair," the woman said. "Sit yourself down, darlin'." A small coffee table stood in front of the rocker. I hadn't noticed that, either. Now I wondered if I had lost my mind. I put my RC and jelly roll on the table.

The woman smiled and said, "Got me a scary story to tell you today, Amanda."

I wanted to ask her how she knew my name, but she cut me off, saying, "Honey, it's a storyteller's job knowing things. You just sit right on back now. Savor your snack whilst I tell you all about the Butler Mansion Tragedy."

I felt a shiver go down my back. The Butler Mansion? That's what our house was called. The real estate lady told us the first owner of our house was a banker named Butler. I remembered when Mom joked, "As in Rhett Butler from *Gone with the Wind*?" Now my interest piqued.

Before I opened my mouth, she nodded her head. "Yes, Amanda, that was the name of the home you now occupy. So, give me your undivided attention. What you seek may be found in the story I'm about to tell."

Outside, the sun began to hide behind dark clouds. I heard thunder in the distance. A strong wind gusted ahead of the storm, blowing against the house and causing me to shiver even more. A part of me wanted to run. Another part froze in anticipation.

The old woman's voice sounded strong and commanding when she started her story with, "A young girl died a tragic death in that old mansion. It was the result of pride and vanity—and evil possession."

Her hands rested on her knees, covering up some of the print flowers of her calico dress, golden sunflowers mixed with crimson mums and deep blue pansies. She reminded me of a pioneer woman. I couldn't wait to hear the story.

25

A Tale of Two Sisters

Her story took place around 1900, she explained. "Two sisters, twin sisters, one animated as the morning sun, the other dark and angry as midnight. Wasn't their faces, honey, made them different. Uh uh, not a'tall. They had the same faces. Both were darling pretty girls, grew to lean, handsome women, dark hair, green eyes, high, sharp cheekbones. No, it wasn't their appearance. It was how they looked out on life.

"Susie, one named Susie, woke up mornings and smiled at the light of day. Maggie, the dark one, stayed in bed and cursed the sunshine. But if that weren't enough, the day arrived when her darkness grew deeper. Was the day Susie announced her engagement. To be wed, she was. To be married and Maggie had no prospects on the horizon."

The old woman smiled at me. "Nowadays," she said, "marriage ain't near important to a young lady as them days. Them days, we called a woman not married before thirty an old maid, a spinster. Was a shame not to be married. Worse shame for Maggie 'cause it was her own darkness kept suitors away. No gentleman caller wanted the hand of a mean-spirited girl. Not one. So, Maggie, when she heard of Susie's wedding plans, she sat right down and brooded. If she couldn't have a husband, she didn't want Susie to have one neither."

A clap of thunder made me jump in my chair. Rain started falling and it got darker, dark as Maggie's heart, I decided.

"What did she do?" I heard myself ask the old storyteller. I could feel the chill from the storm and put my arms across my body to keep warm.

The storyteller shook her head. "She plotted murder, that's

what she done. Plotted the death of her very own sister. But she needed help. That's why she stole off one night, one moonless night, the night before Susie's wedding, stole off to visit the very witch of Dead Scotsman's Holler."

"The witch?" I whispered. I had heard some of the older kids brag they had actually seen her in the hollow. I always thought they lied. It had never occurred to me that the stories could ever have been more than just campfire tales. I heard the question escape my mouth, "She's real? The witch is for real?"

"Yes, darlin', a witch. And not a fair fortune-teller who weaves magic charms for the homely girls in need of love. No, for sure not the fair white witch, but the black lady of Dead Scotsman's Holler, who haunts the nights with evil potions and dark spells, who still lives, some say, hundreds of years after she fled her highland homeland for fear of being burned at the stake."

Outside, a cat screamed. I shivered.

The storyteller's eyes grew narrow. She said, "So it was that Maggie entered the witch's shack and stood there proud, announcing to the shriveled woman, 'Do you have a potion to kill my sister? If you do, I must have it!'

"And the witch said, 'I have all potions. But I demand something in return.'

"Maggie said, 'Whatever you ask, I will pay the price.'

"'Then you will do as I command you, nothing more, nothing less.'"

The old storyteller eased forward and looked into my eyes. "Are you prepared to hear the rest, darlin'?"

I took a deep breath and nodded my head.

"Very well, then, this is what happened next: The witch produced two jeweled mirrors from a dark wooden chest she had concealed under her bed. She told Maggie that a woman named Mary had once owned the two mirrors. So her images were captured in the looking glasses. Happens sometimes, it does. Magic, I suppose. How a mirror can take on a life of its own. How a mirror can capture the very image of the one using it."

"But you said images, I said. "That means two, right?"

"Clever girl," the storyteller said. "Yes, images. You see, the queen had been a powerful woman, a lady of intrigue, and a ruler not above the use of violence to achieve her desires. For a time, whenever she looked into her mirror, she saw the evil person many called Bloody Mary, who had killed and made war to suit her ambitions.

"Then, she was imprisoned. For seventeen years, she planned to escape, sought ways to return to power. All the time, watching her beauty fade as she looked into the same mirror that held her evil image. But her escape plans failed and she was finally sentenced to death by beheading. And that is when the second mirror came into play."

"I had read there were two," I said. "You are talking about Mary, Queen of Scots, aren't you?"

The storyteller said, "Yes, darlin'."

"Then tell me about the second mirror."

"On the eve of her execution, a present arrived for her. From whom? No one ever knew. But since it was a jeweled mirror, an exact copy of the one she owned, her jailer allowed her to have the present. And on that night she looked into the mirror and saw another face. Not the face of a hardened old woman known as Bloody Mary, but the face of a woman able to confess her evil and ask for forgiveness. And so she did pray to be forgiven, and she died in the morning, a look of peacefulness on her face.

"Having explained all this to Maggie, the witch commanded her, 'Take these mirrors with you this night. One for you. One for your sister.' Of course, you can imagine which mirror was intended for the evil Maggie.

"Then the witch went to a cabinet and drew out a package of scented bath salts. She said, 'Take this, too, as a gift to the one you wish to die. The scent will follow her into eternity.'

"In the morning, Maggie woke Susie from her sleep and said she had brought her some special wedding presents—a set of jeweled mirrors and a package of scented bath salts. 'This one here is yours,' Maggie said, handing Susie the mirror of forgiveness, 'and this one is mine. Whenever you look into the mirror, I want you to think of your loving sister. And I, of course, will think of you when I look into the twin mirror.'"

"Then she killed her?" I asked.

The storyteller arranged the hem of her dress and made herself more comfortable on the side of the bed. She held her head high when she said, "Certainly not, darlin'. She would have been caught had she simply strangled her sister, or stabbed her, or hacked her to death with a wood ax. No, no, no! Maggie was much more creative with her evil doings. She watched and waited till Susie took her bath in preparation for the wedding.

"She could hear Susie pour the buckets of water heated from the woodstove into the fancy galvanized bathtub. She listened to her sing whilst she poured the scented bath salts into the water. She waited for Susie to lower herself into the warm, sweet-smelling tub and close her eyes in the comfort of the soothing water.

"That's when Maggie crept into the bathroom, every step touching lightly to the floor so as not to give herself away. When she finally stood over her sister, looking down at her from the back of the tub, she started to shaking. Had to tell herself it would be easy. Just hold her head under the water until she stopped struggling."

The storyteller looked at me and said, "You can breathe now."

I realized I'd been holding my breath and took a big one.

"Wow," I said, "so she killed her own sister?"

The old woman smiled. "Of course not, Amanda. Plans seldom pan out the way a body wants them to. Maggie pondered on it, mighty heavy, to drown her sister. Yes, indeed, she contemplated killing Susie. But she lost her very own nerve and just at that very moment, Susie opened her eyes and saw Maggie. She smiled and said, 'Oh, sister, this is the most wonderful-smelling bath soap. I love you, my dear Maggie.'"

"Then she didn't kill her," I said, "but I thought...."

"You thought this was a story about murder," the storyteller said.

I nodded. "Yes, isn't that what you said at the beginning?"

She smiled at me and said, "I said tragedy, not murder. Be that as it may, there's more than one way to kill a body.

You see, Amanda, Maggie killed her sister in her very own imagination. Of course when Susie saw Maggie standing over her, next to the bathtub, Maggie wouldn't have been able to finish the foul deed. But in fact, it was because of Maggie that Susie died violently that morning."

I said, "Gosh, how?"

The storyteller closed her eyes like she was remembering. Then she opened them and said, "Soon as Maggie left the bathroom, Susie stood up to towel off, and slipped on the soap scum in the tub. She slipped and cracked her head on the side of the fancy galvanized bathtub. Knocked herself flat unconscious. In a matter of minutes, she was dead. Drowned because of the very bath soap her sister gave her as a wedding present.

"When Maggie heard the commotion, she rushed into the room and saw her sister lying there in the tub. Maybe she could have saved her, maybe not. Maybe Susie was already dead by the time it took for Maggie to come back into that bathroom. But don't matter, 'cause you know what Maggie did?"

I shook my head.

"Maggie turned around and took herself out of that lavatory there like nothing had happened."

I said, "Oh, gross!"

The storyteller leaned over toward me and whispered, "So you see, Amanda, whether Maggie killed Susie for sure, or not, ain't important. What's important is that she didn't lift a finger to help her."

That was a horrible story. But now my attention was on the two mirrors in the story. *Was it true what the storyteller said about the witch's giving Maggie the mirrors?* I wondered. *And can the evil mirror really turn someone into Bloody Mary?*

"That's for you to find out, young lady," the storyteller said.

"How do you do that?" I asked.

"Do what, Amanda?"

"How do you know what I'm thinking?"

Her blue eyes twinkled. "There's more to the story," she said. "You do want to hear the rest of it, don't you?"

"Yes, please." The rain had all but stopped. A few drops pattered here and there on the tin roof. It was still dark outside. The wind had died down, and I could smell the freshness of the earth outside, and something else…something almost as fresh and clean, like bath salts—the scent of lilacs.

The storyteller took a deep breath herself and smiled like she also appreciated the way the world smells after it rains.

"Now to finish the story," she said. "Maggie never regretted her sister's death. No one found out. Everyone assumed it was an accident. But as Maggie grew older, she became fascinated with the mirrors, the twin mirrors she briefly shared with her dead sister.

"She would go into the attic to be alone and to look at herself. Whenever she looked into the mirror that belonged to her sister, she saw herself and nothing else. But when she looked into the one she had kept for herself, she saw a dark face, the face of an evil person. It wasn't long before she spent all her time looking into the mirrors, first one, then the other. Finally, when she discovered she was losing her mind, she hid the dark, evil mirror, and kept the one belonging to Susie. Some say that Maggie had turned into a witch herself. Some say that was the price she had to pay the witch of Dead Scotsman's Holler for the bath salts and the mirrors."

The old storyteller drank the last of her water and handed me the glass. "Another tumbler of water, please."

I walked over to the bed and took her glass. It still felt cold, tiny beads of water dripping down the outside of the glass like raindrops on a windowpane. "What finally happened to the wicked sister?" I asked her. "How did she die?"

The storyteller shook her head. "She didn't die, Amanda. She's still alive. When her parents passed away, she inherited the mansion. Lived there alone, allowed no one to visit, remained alone all those years. Then, when she became too old to manage by herself, she placed the mansion up for sale and moved away. But she hasn't died; not yet. She's ancient—over a hundred years old—but not dead. Oh no, Amanda, Maggie Butler is very much alive, and perhaps as much a witch as the woman who helped her kill her very own sister.

"That, my dear, is the price she had to pay for her evil. For you see, the witch knew the truth of it. No one ever commits an evil and walks away free of the guilt. Oh, no, darlin'. Maggie belongs to the witch now, for as long as her deed goes unforgiven."

I asked, "Did she take the good mirror with her when she moved?"

"Wouldn't you take something so valuable, young lady? Wouldn't you keep such a treasure?"

I nodded.

She said, "I have a powerful thirst. Please, more water. Fetch me another tumbler."

26

Pioneer Woman

When I walked into the kitchen, I could smell the bath salts again. "Like the ghostly scent in my hallway at night," I whispered.

I opened the icebox and my mouth dropped open. It was empty. No water pitcher, no soda, no ice that had been there before, not even water in the drip tray where the ice would have melted. I turned back to the stove. No heat radiated from its black cast-iron body. I heard myself say, "But it was warm the last time...."

When I returned to the bedroom, she was gone. The bed was unruffled. There wasn't a trace of anyone who had been there moments before. Even the yellow metal patio rocker was missing, the coffee table too, and my drink and the scrap of jelly roll I hadn't eaten. I looked around. Nothing. Everything gone.

Run, I thought. The scary part of me said, *Run*, but the logical part said, *No, don't be ridiculous. There must be an explanation.* I walked out of the house, down the wood plank walk, and across the yard to the museum office where a receptionist greeted visitors and answered the phone. She was my mom's age, brown hair, dressed in a granny dress, wearing an old-fashioned bonnet. She smiled when I walked up to her desk.

"May I help you?" she said.

My throat felt dry, but I forced out the words, "Can you tell me where the storyteller is?"

The look on her face said something I didn't want to hear. "You must mean the superintendent," she said.

I knew how stupid I must have sounded when I said, "No, the old lady storyteller, the one with the calico dress and hair put up in a bun."

She smiled and for a moment I was sure she understood. "Oh, I get it," she said. "Over in the next hallway," she pointed down a corridor. "You'll find her there."

I was so relieved, my feet ran down the hall even though my mind told me to walk. When I arrived, there was no one around. The hallway was empty except for old black and white photographs, framed and hanging along the wall. I turned around, thinking I had misunderstood the reception-ist's directions. That's when I saw her again.

She looked me straight in the face, still wearing the calico dress, her hair put up, her arms and legs thick as tree trunks, and her chin held high and proud.

The caption under the black and white photograph read, "Pioneer woman. Name unknown."

I thought, *Wait till Dad sees this.* Then I thought, *Uh oh! I must really be losing it.*

27

The Witch

I was sure the librarian would pass out. Amanda Terry at the library twice in one day. I asked her if there was a book written about our town.

"You mean like a history book?" she asked.

"Yes, please," I said. I was prepared to be disappointed, but when she directed me to the section on state history, I was surprised to find several books written about the town where I grew up. The only problem was I wasn't sure I would find what I was looking for.

"Awright!" the library echoed with my voice. Oops. I felt like crawling into a corner. Me and my big mouth. Everyone looked in my direction. No hiding. The red in my face gave me away.

I found it in a tattered book, a picture of my house, the Butler Mansion. Standing on the front porch, Mr. and Mrs. Butler and their twin daughters Maggie and Susie stood solemn-faced, looking at me looking at them. The caption went on to say, "...a tragic accident took the life of Susie Butler. Legend has it her ghost haunts the mansion."

"No kidding," I said, again loud enough that the librarian sitting behind her desk shook her head and held her finger to her lips. I mouthed the words *I'm sorry* and went back to the book.

There was nothing else about the house or the people who lived there. Nothing about the accident, only the mention of a ghost.

I looked at the mansion again. It looked different from the way it was now. There were no neighbors then, and the front porch hadn't been extended around the side of the house. A few tiny trees grew in the front yard. I thought of the tall pecan and walnut trees that make the house seem so dark even during the day. By this time of the year, many of the leaves had fallen, and I was sure the attic would seem less scary than when we first moved into the house.

The mysterious storyteller had told me that Maggie was still alive. A light went on in my head. The phone book!

I found it along with other directories in the reference section. There were eleven Butlers: Aiyana, Andrew Patrick, Cody, Daniel Patrick, Julianne Marie, Katy, London Marie, Margaret Anne, Rhett (Rhett?), Victor Wayne, and Wylma Jean.

No Maggie. I went through the directory again. Maybe she had an unlisted number, or maybe she didn't even have a phone. Or could she have left the city altogether?

Maggie, I thought. *Such an old-fashioned name.* No one at my school was named Maggie. I wondered if it could be a nickname. Back to the computer. *Gosh*, I thought, *the library is like a magic house of knowledge.* This time I didn't even have to ask the librarian. I punched the word *Maggie* into the computer.

Three pages of references and a note at the top of the list which said, "also check reference under name, MARGARET."

Ohhh! Like Margaret...Anne!

Cool, I thought, *this could change the entire direction of detective work.* I was hooked. Back at the phone book I found the address and phone number of Margaret Anne Butler. You should have seen the size of my eyes when I saw the address, 101 Stevens Street.

"That's right around the corner from my house," I said. Suddenly my heart stopped. There was only one occupied house around the corner on Stevens Street, the fallen-down shack of an old woman we kids called the witch.

28

The Ghost

The witch was really Maggie Butler? Worse than that, I was pretty sure I would have to borrow Maggie Butler's mirror—the one she kept after her sister died—if I was going to break the spell that turned Juli into Bloody Mary. But I would need help. My plan was to find a way to get into the witch's home and borrow the mirror. My conscience said I shouldn't do it because the mirror, if it still existed, belonged to Maggie—or more properly, Margaret Anne Butler. But what if I could borrow it and return it?

Confused again. This was not going to be easy. Maybe I could buy it from her? But how? Nobody goes up to a witch and says, "By the way, I need to borrow something from you."

I needed help. It was Saturday. I wouldn't see Ms. Breeze till Monday. There was no one else I felt I could trust. I told myself I should sleep on it, and maybe I would find an answer in the morning.

That night, I had a hard time falling asleep. Just as I drifted off, I thought I smelled the scent of flowers. *Sweet dreams*, I thought. Was I ever right!

It was the middle of the night when singing woke me up.

Couldn't Mom and my stepdad hear it? No. I could hear them snoring loudly as ever. My imagination again? I put on my robe and stepped out into the hallway. The singing seemed clearer now. I stepped toward the stairs. The sound became faint. Downstairs? No, not downstairs. The attic. The singing definitely came from the attic.

My first thought was to wake Mom. I shook my head. It was my problem. I could hear Ms. Breeze: *There are problems you must solve yourself, Amanda.* Besides, I knew they wouldn't believe me, singing or no singing.

I turned and walked toward the attic stairs. The closer I got, the clearer the singing. The song was familiar, though I couldn't remember hearing it before. The stair steps creaked as usual, but the singing didn't stop. When I reached the door, I put my ear against it and listened. It was an eerie song, one that echoed around the attic like a melody in the wind:

> Try to sleep my baby girl,
> Though the night winds whip and whirl,
> Peace will come to you one day,
> You'll be free to run and play.
> Close your eyes and let's pretend,
> We can fly upon the wind,
> To a place far far away,
> From the pain you feel today.

Was I scared? Not me. I was terrified! Slowly, I started to back down the stairs. Halfway, I turned and was about to run for it when I heard the door creak open behind me. I stopped, wanted to turn and look, but couldn't. You might say my body was frozen in fright. Finally, I found the strength and took another step down, praying I wouldn't be jumped by whatever had opened the door behind me.

My foot had just touched the next step when a voice said, "Don't go away. Please don't leave me. I've had no one to play with for such a long time."

This isn't happening, my mind said.

"Please come and play with me," the voice said again. "Promise, I won't hurt you."

I took a deep breath and turned around. No one was there.

Oh no, I thought, *not another dream.* I was about to go back down the stairs when I heard the singing. It was louder now that the door was open.

What do you have to lose? I asked myself.

"Don't answer that," I whispered.

As soon as I stepped into the attic, I could smell the flowers. "Just like bath salts," I said. It was dark so I reached over to my left to flip on the light switch.

"That's not necessary," the voice said. "Just close your eyes and imagine what I must look like."

"Why not?" I mumbled with my eyes closed, "I seem to be able to imagine everything else."

At first, all I saw was the dark, but after a few seconds, a light started to glow in my mind, dimly at first, then stronger little by little. Soon, a shadow emerged from the light. At first it had no form, but after a while I was sure it was girl—a girl smaller than me.

Keep trying, I said to myself. *Keep your eyes shut.* The light became stronger, and the girl came out of the shadows as the eyes of my imagination adjusted to the light. I could picture her features now, the clothes she wore, even the smile on her face.

She was younger than me. Her dress was old-fashioned, white with lots of ribbons and embroidery and lace around the collar and hem. Her long, brown hair was wavy, and it had been tied with a flowing pink ribbon. She had bangs to the top of her brown eyes. She danced around the room in high-topped shoes that laced halfway up her calves. They were shiny black, and I knew if I wore shoes like hers I would want to dance too. In her arms, she held a delicate china doll with its hair and features painted on. I secretly wanted one just like her. When the little girl smiled, her eyes sparkled, and she said, "You can open your eyes now."

I did, and she was there.

29

Forgiveness

I don't recall how long we played. Even though I was older than she was, we played like we were the same age. It was as if I had gone back to the time when playing was the most important thing in my life. To be honest, I didn't want it to end. Even if it seemed only a dream, a part of me said it would be okay for this dream to go on forever.

Her toys were different from the ones I played with. The dolls weren't as lifelike as the ones I had, but they were more magical in some ways. Their clothes were intricate and delicate. No plastic anywhere. The cribs had rubber wheels and looked so real I wondered if a doll put inside one wouldn't suddenly turn into a real baby.

The little girl showed me her miniature people who lived in a tiny toy town. When we played with them, they moved and acted out whatever the little girl and I would fantasize. If I pretended something, it would happen. I felt as if I had been taken back in time. In my mind, I was a little girl again, playing out my daydreams with toys that responded to my every thought. It was so real. Little flakes of snow fell from nowhere, and I was sure I could feel the cold when I reached down to touch the places and people.

"It's our town," she said. "See, here's our house, up here on the hill just beyond the city limits. This town was a Christmas present from Father. He said Santa had it built specially for me and...." She couldn't say the name, but I knew she meant Maggie.

We were in the middle of tea, a delicate China service just her size, when she looked over my shoulder and said, "I must go soon."

I looked behind me and saw the tiniest hint of the dawn through the attic window. "Do you have to?" I asked.

She smiled. "I've had the most wonderful time since...since I died."

I felt a blast of wind blow across my face, and I shivered. The window to the attic wasn't open. I knew the wind had not come from my world. "Can we play again?" I asked her.

She shook her head. "I would rather you do me a favor."

"I will if I can," I said.

She reached out to touch me, and I realized ghosts can't be felt even if they can be seen or, in my case, dreamed. She must have understood this too, because I thought I saw a tear in the corner of her eye. She looked down, then squared her shoulders and looked me straight in the face.

"I want you to tell someone that I forgive her," she said.

A chill went down my spine. "You mean your sister, don't you?" I said.

She nodded. "When I died, I was very angry at her. She could have saved me, you see. But my anger lasted only a short while. Then a wonderful thing happened. I was allowed to return to a younger age when it's very easy to forgive. You're still young, Amanda. Before long, you, too, will lose your need for magic, and other things will become more important. Those are the years when many of us forget how to forgive."

I wanted to say I'd never get that old, but I wondered if she knew things I could not understand.

She nodded as if she could read my mind. "Forgiveness is a gift of children. When people grow up they settle their differences in other ways—lawsuits, wars, meanness. Many lose their freedom to forgive because they harden their hearts and keep hatred inside themselves. It eats at them until they are worse than the ones they hate. Can you see how important it is that Maggie knows I have forgiven her?"

I shrugged my shoulders. "But you seem so happy," I said. "Why is it so important to you?"

"It is not for me, Amanda, it is important for her. I want her to be free, and she cannot let go of the ugliness in her life until she knows how much I still love her."

I said, "You want me to tell her...."

"That I forgive her, that's all."

"But it's like she got away with murder!" The words blurted out of my mouth before I could stop them. Maybe it was the frustration I felt knowing I lived in a world where kids kill kids, and I realized the ugliness of it ached inside me like a sickness.

She sensed my anger. "No one gets away with murder, Amanda. No one. Taking a life is never free. It robs the killer of innocence, takes the smile out of a heart, and dulls the excitement of playing in a running stream or watching snowflakes fall from the sky. There are some, like Maggie, who become insane with guilt and the fear of being discovered. And only forgiveness can make it better." She sighed. "Sometimes, not even that."

"I want to understand," I said.

"I know you do, Amanda, that's why I allowed you to visit with me today."

I shook my head. *Too bad this is only a dream*, I said to myself as I turned to the window. The red light of dawn slipped through the shutters. It was easier for sunshine to enter the attic now that the leaves had fallen from the trees. When I turned back, she was gone. The attic looked as it had when I first saw it. No beautiful toys, no miniature town, no Susie playing with her dolls.

Yes, you have been dreaming again, I said to myself.

I felt sad, and wished it had been more than a dream.

30

A Special Gift

No one was awake when I walked down the hall to my room. I closed the door behind me and snuggled into bed. My eyes closed and I could see Susie again and the beautiful porcelain doll she first held in her arms. "What a wonderful dream it was," I whispered.

When I opened my eyes, bright sunlight splashed across the ceiling, and Mom was sitting on the bed next to me.

She smiled and said, "Do you plan to sleep forever?"

I smiled back and brought my arms over my head to stretch. It felt good.

"Where did you get this?" Mom said. She reached down by my side and picked up something snuggled next to me. "This is beautiful, Amanda." She examined it, then her eyes narrowed and I wondered if I would be in trouble again.

"Where did you get this?" she asked again.

I recognized it immediately but couldn't answer right away. How could I explain a gift from someone who didn't exist?

Mom held Susie's china doll, features and hair painted on her head, clothes intricate and delicate.

"It used to be Susie's," I said. "She must have known how much I wanted it."

Before she could ask me who Susie was, I said, "Mom, there's something really important I have to do today."

She smiled again and said, "That's nice, honey."

Mom was still puzzled. She couldn't take her eyes off the china doll.

I couldn't take my mind off the little girl who had left it for me.

31

The Messenger and the Witch

Ever hear the phrase, *Kill the messenger?*

Maggie Butler didn't wait for the message. She jerked open the door and raged at me through the screen, "Go away, you filthy child! Go away before...."

I didn't wait to hear the before what. You wouldn't believe a girl my age could long jump as far as I did.

It was Sunday afternoon. I told Mom I was going to visit Jessica. I didn't tell her I was going to see Jessica after I made a stop at the witch's house. Even during the day, the old house looked dark and foreboding. It was the only occupied house on the block, if you could call it a block. All the other houses were abandoned and boarded up. Hers sat up against the side of a scrubby hill.

The witch's house was covered by scraggly hackberry and oak trees, which grew every which way, shrouding the house like a dark green cloud in the summer and a twisted vine monster in the winter. I had never even gotten close to the house. We kids would dare each other to go up and knock on the door. I guess I was the first one who did.

When I jumped off the porch the first time I tried her house, I got my socks, jeans, and sweatshirt so full of thistles I felt like a human porcupine. I must admit I had to ask myself if I really had lost it when I decided to go back a second time. This time, though, I was more determined. After all, what more could she do to me than yell and scream? I decided not to answer that question.

Instead of knocking, I stood on the porch and yelled, "Miss Butler, I have a message for you. Really I do, please."

For a while it was quiet. My mind was made up. She would have to listen to me this time. An icy breeze blew across the porch. Fall had banked up against the side of the shaded hill. Everything smelled like rotten wood and mold. I sneezed, and a shrill, high-pitched voice said, "Bless you."

I jumped high enough to touch the porch ceiling. When I landed, the witch appeared, watching me from behind the rusted screen door.

"Well?" was all she said.

"I have a message for you." I tried to keep my voice from breaking with fear.

"You already said that." Her voice sounded tired and impatient, but not really like a witch. She hadn't cackled or snickered or anything. Not yet, anyway.

I was prepared for the worst when I said, "It's from Susie."

There was a long pause. I could barely make out her face for the screen and darkness of the house.

Finally, she spoke, her voice just above a whisper, "Come in."

She walked away, and I stood there not yet able to make my arm reach for the door. The floorboards creaked as she moved away. When I finally grabbed the handle to open the screen door, I could hear a slow rhythmic creak I recognized as a rocking chair. The door opened easily and I stepped inside.

The room had a peculiar odor, one I never smelled before. It was not sweet, not unpleasant, but different, sort of like the inside of an old closet.

She sat in the rocker, pushing back and forth, her head down, thin bony fingers grasping the arms. Her hair, almost white, hung down into her lap. She wore a dark wool dress, a gray knitted shawl, and tattered house slippers.

The room was cold and damp. Thick drapes covered the windows. I looked for someplace to sit. No chair, only her rocker and telephone table. The woman began to lift her head and I was prepared to be afraid. I was surprised to find I wasn't.

Her face was long and thin, but not ugly. Her skin was wrinkled and her eyes dim, almost colorless. She did not smile at me, but neither did she scowl. "You have a message for me?" she said.

I saw no reason to beat around the bush. "Susie says she forgives you."

She said nothing and I wondered out loud, "You don't seem surprised."

I thought I almost saw a smile sneak across her lips. It did not last long. She said, "I've waited over eighty years to hear from her." Her eyes began to water, but she did not cry. "You may leave now," she said.

My instinct was to turn and get out of there as fast as I could. But I had a mission. I was not going to wait more than eighty years to help my stepsister, Juli.

"I need something," I said.

She didn't answer at first, and I was prepared for another outburst. But it didn't come. Instead, she lifted herself from the rocker and said, "I'll return in a moment." When she came back, she had the mirror in her hand.

"How did you know?" I asked.

Her voice was a whisper now, but this time she seemed to speak with kindness. "I should have destroyed the evil twin mirror when I left home," she replied, "but I did not have the courage. My spell can be lifted only when another person is bewitched. Then alone can the spell be broken by someone purer than me. If Susie has chosen you, then you must be the one to break the spell.

"This mirror is my only treasure. It is the key that unlocks the spell. But, beware, child. The evil spirit will not give up easily. You must outwit her. I know this because she is me. She is the evil I allowed to possess me, and until she is changed, the evil will endure. This mirror has the power of good, Susie's power. But it must be wielded cleverly, or the monster will destroy it. Beware, child, the evil must be out-witted."

That was the first and last time I saw the witch. She had given me her most valued possession, the power of good. I would have to use it soon. Next Saturday was Juli's Halloween party. I was sure Bloody Mary would be invited.

32

You'll Think of Something

I apologized to Ms. Breeze. "One more week. Please give me one more week and I'll be back to my normal lazy self."

I arrived at school early, and she suspected I wanted to talk. "I take it you've made some headway on your monster problem." She said it like she meant it, not a hint of talking down to me like some adults do to kids when they don't believe them.

I said, "I saw the ghost who haunts our house, and she sent me to her sister who is known as a witch, but who really isn't because she gave me the mirror which will reverse the spell that made Juli into Bloody Mary."

Ms. Breeze said, "Cool! Now can you run that by me again, one at a time?"

We talked for almost half an hour. I did most of the talking. Ms. Breeze listened. When I got to the part where the ancient Maggie Butler gave me the mirror, Ms. Breeze said, "Cool!" again. I told her I still hadn't figured out how to make Juli say "Bloody Mary" into the new mirror in the dark. She said I'd find a way.

I needed her trust. Kids can't always depend on grownups to get them out of fixes, but it feels really good when the grownups believe in us anyway. When the bell rang for classes to start, she said, "Amanda, I'm almost jealous. Adults lose all the magic in their lives and don't get the chance to fight monsters. I'm sure if I tried to help you, I would mess it up because I've lost touch with the special way kids solve their problems. I'll do what I can. I'm pulling for you, kiddo."

She called me *kiddo.* I never heard her say that to anyone before. I told myself it was a special word she used for children she felt close to. I wondered if other teachers knew how important it was for the kids they taught to feel their teachers cared for them. It's wonderful to feel special.

On Saturday morning I didn't feel all that special. Dad was coming, and I wondered if I had a good enough plan for Bloody Mary. *Oh well,* I said to myself, *you'll find out soon enough.*

It was October 31—Halloween.

33

Preparations

I've always loved parties. Birthday parties, slumber parties, pool parties, it didn't matter to me. But this party, I was sure, would be the party I would remember for the rest of my life. I hoped that would be a long, long time.

Juli was the picture of politeness. She looked almost surprised to see me drive up with Dad. She met me at the garage door and gave me a big hug. "I wasn't sure you'd be able to make it," she said.

I said, "I wouldn't have missed it for anything."

She smiled and led me into the kitchen where her mom was busy preparing the cake and cookies. "Wash your hands, both of you, and get over here," Kay said.

We actually had fun, playing with—I mean rolling—the dough, getting flour all over our faces, hair, and clothes, and laughing like we always did when we had a project. My mom and Juli's mom make work fun. Of course, this time Kay did have to yell at us when we got out of control, but she always found something funny even when we messed up, like when Juli dropped some of the cookie dough on the floor and I stepped on it. Squish! "Oh yuck!" I said. We laughed so hard I started to cry.

By the time the cookies were done and the cakes were in the oven, it was getting dark. We snacked on cookies and some cheese and lunch meats Kay had arranged for the guests. There would be seven in all: Juli and me and five of her best friends. Everyone was to wear the most hideous, grotesque costume she could create. I knew what Juli would look like, but she didn't know how I would dress. It was going to be an enormous surprise.

Ms. Breeze helped me make it. She had some experience as a costume designer for her college drama department. It took us all week to put it together. I was sure it would be a hit, especially with Juli.

"Time to get ready," Juli's mom said.

I said, "I know, why don't we all dress in different rooms so we can surprise each other."

"Cool!" Juli said. "Way awesome idea! Bet I'll be the most surprised."

I smiled at her and said, "I'm sure you will, Juli. I'm sure you will."

34

Surprise

"Everybody ready?" Juli's mom yelled from the bathroom where she had changed into her costume. I was in the bedroom across from the bathroom, and Juli was in the one next to mine.

"I need a few more minutes," I yelled.

Juli's mom said, "Amanda, you're so slow! God will probably grow old waiting for you to die."

"I sure hope so," I whispered to myself. But she was right. Being slow was something I didn't have to work at. My mom dreaded taking me out to eat because I ate so slowly. My stepdad's face always got red in restaurants because I seemed to take three times as long to eat my food as he did his. Mom would just fidget and say, "Aren't you through yet?"

My own dad didn't seem to mind as much. He always said kids who eat slowly digest their food better and don't gain as much weight later on. Of course, when he takes me out to eat, he sometimes makes me put my food in a doggie bag and eat it in the car on the way home.

Getting into my costume took time because it was so complicated. Ms. Breeze put together special makeup including false teeth, skin texture, and contact lenses tinted and painted to change the way my eyes looked. That was just the beginning. By the time I put on the rest of the costume and looked in the mirror, I scared even myself. Boy, was Juli going to be surprised.

I yelled, "Ready or not, here I come."

Juli's mom said, "Okay, let's all come out of our rooms at the same time. Ready...NOW!"

We stepped out into the hall together. Juli's mom looked like an old man, a dead one. She wore a black dress and cape and carried a broom handle with a cardboard replica of a sickle on it. She was obviously Mr. Death. When she saw Juli and me, she screamed.

Juli was Bloody Mary, looking the way only Bloody Mary could look: bent over, wearing an old flannel nightgown and a dark bathrobe. Her hair was long and matted, and she had dark curly hair on her arms. Her fingers were long and bony, and her fingernails were twisted, long, and sharp. But it was her face that was truly horrible. It was wrinkled, with blood-shot eyes and a twisted mouth that showed jagged teeth and a black, pocked tongue when she smiled. She was Bloody Mary, and when she looked at me to see who I was, she did the same thing her mother had done—she screamed.

She screamed because I was dressed as...Bloody Mary.

My makeup turned my face into a wrinkled maze of twisted skin. The contact lenses made my eyes green with jagged lines looking like broken blood vessels crisscrossing the yellow of my eyes like a road map. My nose twisted just like Juli's, and I had dipped my tongue in purple food coloring and attached false caps over my teeth, making them every bit as menacing as the real things. The hair on my arms was held in place by rubber cement, and my false hands fit like the rubber gloves they were. Ms. Breeze had made them up specially from latex doctor's gloves which she colored to look like the real things. Then she covered them with black furry hair she had saved from her poodle. Poor Pepper. He had to suffer through another haircut just for me. But it was worth it. Now there were two Bloody Marys, and the real one looked like she didn't know what to make of it.

Juli's mom said, "How in the world did you two ever do that?"

Before anyone had a chance to answer or say anything about the "coincidence," the doorbell rang, and we went to greet our guests.

"SCREEEEEECHHHHHHH!"

They came one at a time, and each time we opened the door, the guest standing there screamed louder. By the time there were six of us, we were sure the last one would pass out.

Hermalinda, the first to arrive, was unrecognizable. She wore a long cloak with a grotesque green tail trailing behind it. Her face was a slimy mass of green monster who looked like a fugitive from a nuclear explosion.

Desiree came as a teenage mutant ninja turtle complete with shell and assorted martial arts weapons. When we opened the door, she assumed a threatening pose and said, "Hiiijaaa," followed by an ear piercing, "eeeeeeeiiiiiiiijjjjjjj-jaaaaahhhhhh!" when she saw us standing there. To be honest, I wondered if maybe she didn't pee her pants—I mean her shell.

Heather looked like a blue blob. I'm not sure how she managed to breathe underneath that stuff which looked like wet funny putty. She tried to scream when we opened the door, but it sounded more like a muffled belch.

Erin was next. She came as the Empire State Building and almost lost her observation tower when she tried to get through the door. I wondered how she planned to eat or sleep in that thing.

Ina Katherine came last. She chose to be an angel. Not the least bit scary, but her wings were so wide, we had to fold them to get her through the front door. Her face was made up to look white with rosy highlights on her cheeks. With the blonde wig and halo, she did look pretty celestial. When she saw the rest of us, I thought she would pass out. She never did have much of a stomach for gore.

We made it downstairs to the basement with a whole lot of effort. The Empire State Building had to slide down with help from the blob at the bottom keeping her from crashing to the floor. The ninja turtle steadied her observation tower.

Ina Katherine, the angel, got her wings caught in the doorway, and we had to perform an operation, removing them till she got downstairs. Juli's mother found a way to reattach them later.

When everyone was in the basement, Juli's mom said, "Let's everyone introduce ourselves. I'll start, then serve the goodies. After we've all eaten, I'll leave you girls, I mean THINGS to yourselves." Kay lowered her voice and tried to imitate a man when she said, "My name is Mr. Death. Beware, or you'll see more of me tonight."

No kidding, I said to myself.

Kay still kept her pretend man's voice and said, "Introduce yourselves girls, I mean gruels." She wanted to be funny but no one laughed.

Heather tried to speak first, but no one could understand her because her voice was still muffled by the blue stuff around her head and body.

Desiree told us she was a Ninja Turtle. No one was surprised.

Ina Katherine said she was the Angel Gabriel. Her sweet voice did sound kind of heavenly.

Hermalinda announced she was the last living velociraptor from Jurassic Park.

Heather, the blob, tried again, and we could finally make out something like, "I'm the Pollution Monster who eats up everything in her way."

Erin was last. She identified herself as the Empire State Building, which everyone had already figured out.

Kay looked at her daughter and said, "You're next, Juli."

No one was prepared for what came next. In a deep, raspy voice that sounded more convincing than anyone else's, Juli said, "I'm Bloody Mary."

You could hear the other girls suck in their breaths. Even Kay seemed to shudder when she heard Juli. Then she laughed it off and said, "Cool! That's pretty good, Juli. Now you, Amanda."

I knew I had to make it good. If this didn't work, nothing would. Using the deepest, scariest voice I could make up, I said, "I'm Bloody Mary, and I'm sooooo hungry. I haven't eaten in a hundred years. I'll gobble your noses and nibble on your ears."

The other girls screamed.

I looked over at the real Bloody Mary. She had a dark, sinister frown on her face. She stared coldly at me, and the look in her eyes screamed murder. Then she smiled and whispered, "We'll see, dearie. We'll see!"

35

Battle of the Monsters

She wouldn't take her eyes off me. I tried to stay away from her by pretending to play with the other girls. But every now and then, we got close to each other, and she would say things like, "Soon, dearie, very soon."

By three o'clock, only the blob, Bloody Mary, and I were still awake. By four, the blob leaned against one of the walls, and after a while, all I could hear was something that sounded like funny putty snoring.

Bloody Mary looked across the room at me and twisted her already crooked mouth into a smile. "Now it's just you and me, dearie," she whispered. She stood on the side of the room next to the extension cord Dad had hooked up earlier so we could have light in the basement.

I knew what she had in mind. I was wrong. I thought she would simply pull the cord out of the socket and kill the light. But monsters never do anything that easy.

Instead, her twisted hand grabbed for the cord, and she took the electric line in her mouth.

"Don't!" I said, "You'll electrocute yourself!"

She laughed, showing more of her awesome teeth, then she bit down as hard as she could. Suddenly, everything went ballistic. It was like a Frankenstein movie. Her long hair stood on end, and there were crackles of electricity and bolts of lightning coming from her mouth. I thought she would scream, but she only laughed and bit down all the harder. Then, in a flash, it went dark. I could smell burned hair and singed monster.

Was she dead? I wondered.

It was as quiet as death.

My heart throbbed. I could feel the sweat bead down my forehead to my face. My makeup burned my eyes. I tried to rub them, but that only made it worse. "Be still, Amanda," I whispered, wondering if Bloody Mary had killed herself.

A sudden burning filled my chest, and I thought I would cry. That would mean Juli was dead, too. I couldn't allow myself to think about it. Is this how Maggie Butler felt when she allowed her sister, Susie, to die? I prayed Juli wasn't dead. In a moment my prayers were answered. Something started to rustle across from me in the direction I last saw Bloody Mary.

A deep, hollow voice whispered, "You shouldn't have pretended to be me, dearie. There's only one Bloody Mary, and when I'm finished eating you, I'll eat the others. You have no idea how hungry I am...."

"You can't do this!" I said. It surprised me how strong my voice sounded. "You're not Bloody Mary. You're my stepsister, Juli, and you're not a killer!"

She groaned. "Juli's dead, my dear, and from the moment I eat you, she will never rise again."

I listened to her movements and tried to gauge where she was. As she moved toward me, I edged away, struggling to keep a safe distance between her and me. Still, with every step, she narrowed the gap between us. I was being herded into a corner. She knew what she was doing.

This time, she would give me no room to run. I knew it wouldn't matter if I screamed. No one would respond to my cries for help. Even if the noise did wake Dad and Kay, they would believe we were only playing. This time, Bloody Mary had me where she wanted me. I was getting closer and closer to the corner where she planned to finish me off.

I tried reasoning with her. "You'll be discovered," I said. "Even if you get away with this, you'll be found out and punished."

She cackled. When she spoke, her voice sounded excited. She was breathing heavily, like an animal getting ready to eat. "I will never be discovered," she said. "Even though Juli will no longer live, I can take her body. No one will believe such an innocent person would do such a thing. She will tell the police a monster did this. And she won't even have to lie." She cackled again.

By then, I was almost in the corner.

She was close now, almost close enough to touch. I could smell her breath again, foul and putrid, telling me she had her mouth open and was about to take a bite out of something. That something was me.

"You're wrong," I whispered. "You can't eat me."

She was standing directly in front of me. I could feel the heat from her body. Her breath blew in my face as she said, "Why not, dearie? You'll make a perfect meal!"

I said, "Because I'm Bloody Mary now. I found a magic mirror and said 'Bloody Mary' thirteen times into it and have the same powers as you." My voice got very strong and confident. I continued, "Can't you see, you fool? Now, I'M BLOODY MARY, and I'm going to eat YOU!"

"What?" It stopped her. There was an edge in her voice which told me she wasn't so sure of herself anymore.

I took the initiative. "Now I'm Bloody Mary so you can forget about your plans for dinner."

She screamed, "NOOOOOOOOOOOO!! There's only one Bloody Mary, ME, you little liar, ME! I'M BLOODY MARY."

There was a self assurance and peacefulness in my voice when I responded, "Yes, Juli, you are Bloody Mary, but you won't be for long. You just said your name in the magic mirror, and soon you will be free."

I continued holding the mirror in my hands. It was immediately in front of me, right in the face of the monster. I had hidden it in the special pocket Ms. Breeze sewed into my costume. I had managed to get the monster to say her name, and made sure the mirror was in front of her horrible face when she did it. This time, it had to work. I was certain. But nothing happened. The room became quiet again. All I could hear was the sound of her breathing in front of me. Suddenly, I wasn't so sure anymore.

I remembered what had happened the last time I got Bloody Mary to say her name in a mirror. That time it didn't work. But this time I had the right mirror. Or did I? Some of my courage began to wane. Would it fail again?

The room stayed silent and seemed to get colder. I couldn't even hear her breathing anymore. In front of me, I could hear nothing. It was as if my words had acted as a shield keeping the monster at bay. But for how long? I waited, trying to keep my body from trembling. A chill ran dawn my spine. Something inside of me said, *If you're wrong, you'll soon be dinner for a monster.*

Suddenly, I sensed a movement in front of me, then I felt her grasp me by the shoulders. She held me firmly in her arms and started to pull me to her.

I screamed hysterically and almost passed out. It didn't work, and now Bloody Mary was going to eat me. I could feel her trembling against me. It was only a matter of time. I didn't have the strength to fight back. Now her face was next to mine, and she pulled me against her and said, "Oh, Amanda, I love you!"

It was Juli! My stepsister Juli! The spell was broken.

Epilogue

Mom said it was wonderful how peaceful I looked when I arrived back from visiting Dad. My stepdad peeked over the top of his newspaper and agreed.

All Ms. Breeze could say was "COOL!" when I told her the story of how Bloody Mary turned back into Juli. She made me promise to write about it one day. Teachers! Always on the lookout for creative expression.

Jessica told me she heard from Josie who said Gerald Grandhopper told her that his uncle (who is an undertaker) said Miss Maggie Butler finally passed away and was buried next to her sister in the town cemetery.

The next time Dad came to pick me up, I asked him to stop at the museum. He agreed when I said I had a surprise for him. You should have seen the look in his eyes when he saw the picture of the unknown pioneer woman.

The mirror?

I still have it.

Who knows what power might still be locked in there for me to use at a later time?